The Girls of Lighthouse Lane

Rose's Story

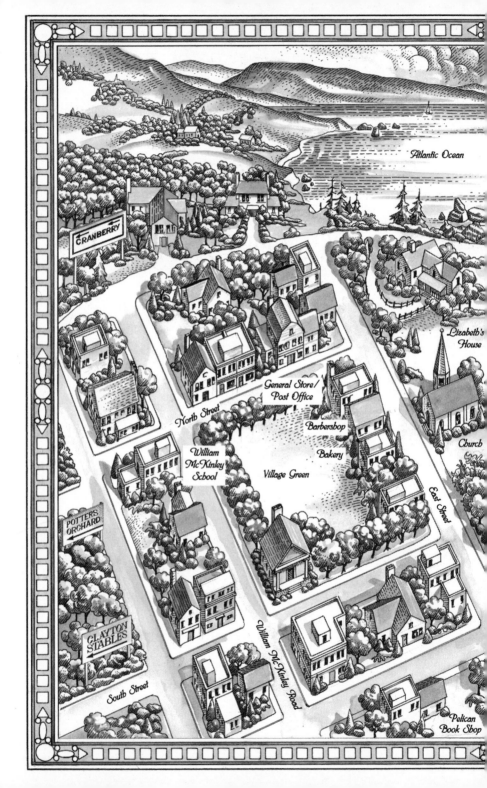

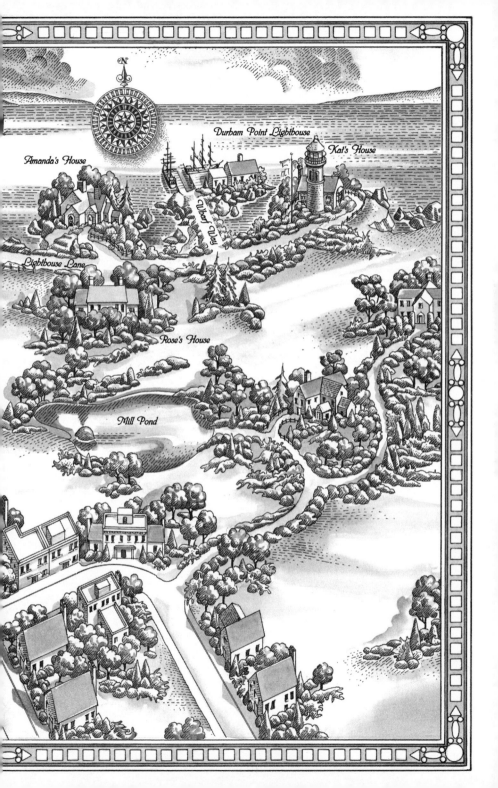

THOMAS KINKADE

The Girls of Lighthouse Lane

Rose's Story

A CAPE LIGHT NOVEL

By Erika Tamar

HarperCollins*Publishers*

A PARACHUTE PRESS BOOK

Library of Congress Cataloging-in-Publication Data
Kinkade, Thomas, 1958-
    Rose's story / by Thomas Kinkade and Erika Tamar. — 1st ed.
        p. cm. — (The girls of Lighthouse Lane ; #2)
    "A Parachute Press book."
    Summary: In 1906, mortified by her mother's suffragist activities that cause
the family to move from New York City to Cape Light, fourteen-year-old Rose
sees no value in her mother's feminist views until she tries to enter a horse-riding
competition open only to boys.
    ISBN 0-06-054344-2 — ISBN 0-06-054345-0 (lib. bdg.)
    [1. Horses—Fiction. 2. Mothers and daughters—Fiction. 3. Suffragists—
Fiction. 4. Friendship—Fiction. 5. Moving, Household—Fiction. 6. Family life—
New England—Fiction. 7. New England—History—20th century—Fiction.]
I. Tamar, Erika. II. Title.
PZ7.K6192Ro 2004   2003056738
[Fic]—dc22   CIP
                                                                 AC

1 2 3 4 5 6 7 8 9 10
❖
First Edition

The Girls of Lighthouse Lane

Rose's Story

❧ *Prologue* ❧

November 10, 1905
New York City

Rose Forbes was flushed with happiness. The most popular group in ninth grade at Miss Dalyrumple's Institute for Young Ladies had accepted her after-school invitation.

"You can leave your schoolbooks on the hall table," Rose said as she led the other six girls inside her Gramercy Park apartment.

Abigail had visited before, but this was the first time the whole crowd had come to her house. Abigail, of course, and Elinor, Margaret, Patience, Claire, and Sue-Ellen.

The maid was standing by with her arms full of their coats. "Bridget, could you please bring us some of those lace cookies?" Rose said. "We'll be in the parlor. Thank you. Oh—and does anyone want hot cocoa?"

Everyone nodded. It was a cold November day and hot cocoa was just perfect, Rose thought. And she'd show them the stereoscope viewer. They'd like that. Later they might gather around the pianola.

She was one of them now! She'd never thought that would happen. In the secret slam book that had been passed around Miss Dalyrumple's, her classmates had written "kind" and "quiet" on Rose's page. Nothing terrible, but she sounded like someone easily forgotten. One of the meaner girls did write, "Rose thinks she's a horse." It was true that sometimes Rose forgot herself and galloped at recess, with her long black hair turning into a flowing mane. But her riding class at the Equestrian Center was the best part of her week, and look how it had turned out—it had led her right into this brand-new popularity!

One day, Abigail Anderson joined Rose's riding class at the Equestrian Center and everything changed. Pretty, self-confident Abigail was always in the center of things at Miss Dalyrumple's. The other girls would crowd around to hear her whispers. Peals of laughter surrounded Abigail. And suddenly, Rose and Abigail had riding in common and lots to talk about! When Abigail decided to include Rose in her group, it was heaven. But Rose liked Abigail most when it was just the two of them poring over Rose's horse scrapbooks and dreaming of having horses of their own one day. Often in front of the others, Abigail could be bossy and sharp-tongued.

Rose showed her new friends into the pretty red parlor. Momma's portrait hung over the marble mantel. It had been painted by an artist-patient of Poppa's, in place of a cash payment. The style suited Momma's long-lashed, huge dark eyes, shining black hair, and ivory skin, all glorious against black velvet.

"Is that your mother?" Claire asked.

"She's *beautiful*," Sue-Ellen breathed. "She doesn't even look like somebody's mother."

Rose felt warm with pride until she felt Abigail staring critically at her.

"You do have the same coloring," Abigail said. "Too bad your features are so different."

Rose had Momma's eyes—Poppa called them flashing gypsy eyes—but she had the Forbes nose, and there wasn't a thing she could do about it. Resentment of Abigail's words simmered inside her.

Abigail had been snappy with Rose all day. At riding class yesterday afternoon Rose had been singled out for praise. But that couldn't be Abigail's reason, Rose thought—could it?

The visit was going well. The girls enjoyed looking into the stereoscope viewer; Rose had hundreds of cards showing foreign countries and exotic people and all sorts of things. It was amazing the way two cards could become a three-dimensional picture that looked so real.

The girls were in the front hall, on the way to Rose's room, when Momma came striding in—straight from a suffragette parade on Fifth Avenue! Rose hadn't expected that; not today! And Momma was wearing *bloomers*! The long, loose trousers that billowed down to tight gathers at Momma's ankles were splattered with fruit stains! Rotten fruit had been thrown at her—Rose could smell it! And a streak of dirt was across Momma's forehead. But instead of looking embarrassed, she was flushed with excitement.

She greeted the girls, shrugged off her appearance, and rambled on about Susan B. Anthony and Elizabeth Cady Stanton. "They're the founders of the voting rights movement," she said, "and I encourage all of you to read their pamphlets. Right here on the hall table—please help yourself. And take some for your sisters, too. The movement needs brave young women just like you." She looked around at their stunned faces and smiled. "Women *will* get the vote one day and we'll just go on demonstrating and protesting until Congress finally makes it a law." Then she laughed prettily, all dimples, and said, "I do think I need a bath! Excuse me, girls."

Six pairs of eyes stared at Momma as she flounced away. Only Rose kept her eyes down. She didn't know where to look. After Momma was out of sight, there was an awful, endless, heavy silence.

Abigail broke it. "That was the *strangest* spectacle I ever saw." Her words dripped acid. "What's wrong with your mother?"

"Nothing!" Rose said. How dare this girl—this girl who was too quick to use her whip when a horse couldn't understand her poor commands—how *dare* she call her sweet, kind, beautiful mother a spectacle!

"Bloomers are disgusting and vulgar!" Abigail looked around at the others, her eyebrows raised. "There has to be something *seriously* wrong with her."

No one talked about Rose's family that way! "There's nothing wrong with my mother! What's wrong with *yours*?"

Abigail's eyes narrowed. There was a gasp from the others.

"Just exactly what do you mean?" Abigail asked icily.

"I don't think you can afford to talk about other

people's mothers when your own staggers about from too much Pinkham's Tonic for Ladies!"

In a flash, Rose knew the wrong words had come tumbling out of her mouth. Mrs. Anderson *did* stagger and she *did* swallow pints of Pinkham's to medicate her "women's troubles." Everyone knew it had exceptionally high alcohol content. But, true or not, Rose wished she could take her words back. It was too late.

❧

An enraged Abigail was a bad enemy to have. Everyone in school followed her lead and they all stopped speaking to Rose. She became invisible—except when people whispered behind their hands and stared at her.

The silent treatment was painful. Rose tried to talk to Abigail about horses again, but Abigail looked past her and through her. And when Rose offered to help Patience with her arithmetic—she'd helped her before and Patience had always been grateful—Patience glanced nervously at Abigail and hissed, "Scat! Leave me alone." It was all Momma's fault.

Rose had nothing against the idea of women getting the vote, but it got people too riled up. Momma could be so charming that some people forgave her eccentricities, but why didn't she stop to think that Poppa was a doctor with a society practice? When word of her antics got out, Poppa's practice, along with dinner invitations, dwindled.

Rose hoped that the Abigail incident would blow over, at least with some of her classmates, and it almost did—Sue-Ellen started acting friendly again. But only a week later, there was a scandal more horrible than anything Rose could have imagined—Momma was arrested! And put in handcuffs like a common criminal! Rose was quite sure Momma was the only Dalyrumple mother who was ever jailed. There was an article in the *New York Daily Mirror* for everyone in New York City to read! Now the Forbes family was avoided by anyone who mattered. In school, Rose became a permanent outcast. Her loneliness felt like a bad disease that knotted her stomach.

When Aunt Norma, Momma's sister, and Uncle Ned came to New York City for their annual Christmas visit, they talked about how badly Poppa's practice had been affected by the scandal.

"Why don't you consider moving to Cape Light?" Uncle Ned asked. "There's a real need for a doctor. The closest one is in Cranberry and that's really too far."

"That could be interesting," Poppa said. "What do you think, Miranda?"

"I don't know," Momma said. "It would be a huge change for us. For one thing, it would mean pulling Rose out of her school."

"I wouldn't mind that at all," Rose said. She had never told her parents about being shunned. It would hurt Momma to know that she'd been the cause of it.

"You liked Cape Light, didn't you, Rose?" Aunt Norma asked.

Rose nodded. She knew that Cape Light was a tiny peninsula in Massachusetts jutting into the Atlantic Ocean. She'd visited there on a one-week vacation back when she was ten. She had discovered riding at Aunt Norma and Uncle Ned's stables. The wonderful Clayton Stables! Otherwise, all she really remembered was the lighthouse that was visible from every part of the town. She'd always wondered what it was like inside.

It would be very strange to live in a small fishing village, but Cape Light could be her escape from Miss Dalyrumple's Institute for Young Ladies.

✥ one ✥

March 19, 1906
Cape Light

"**P**ull it *tighter*, Momma!" Rose inhaled and clutched the bedpost with both hands as her mother laced up her new corset. If she could manage to hold her breath, maybe they could cinch her waist by another inch.

"I'm not about to cut off your air supply," Momma said.

"*Please*," Rose begged. "Only for this morning." Starting at a new school in a new town in the middle of the semester was hard. She had to look her best and acquiring a waistline would certainly help. "Please, Momma. I don't need air!"

"If you can't breathe, you can't think, Rose." Momma smiled. "And you do need a working brain in school, don't you?"

Why did Momma look amused? There was nothing funny about this!

"You've just turned fourteen—why do you feel you have to rush into that awful contraption?" Momma went on.

Easy for *her* to say, Rose thought. Momma had the perfect hourglass figure without even trying! Rose was tall and skinny and absolutely straight up and down. Every move Momma made was graceful. Every move Rose made put her in immediate danger of tripping over her too-big feet. It wasn't fair.

"It's bad enough that grown women are willing to torture their bodies into unnatural shapes, but—"

"All right, all right!" Rose interrupted. Momma was winding up to make one of her speeches and this morning, of all mornings, Rose couldn't bear to hear a word of it.

"—and the restraints of corsets and long, heavy skirts . . . well, as Amelia Bloomer said, that's tied in with denying the vote to women. Keeping them helpless and—"

"I know all about it," Rose muttered. If she never heard the name Amelia Bloomer again, it would be too soon. Sometimes it seemed that the suffragette who wore

pantaloons as everyday outer clothing, of all things, had moved right into their household. How awful to go down in history with *bloomers* named for you, Rose thought, even if they were supposed to give women freedom of movement. Though Miss Bloomer had died in 1894, more than ten years ago, Momma quoted her every other day!

"You know that corsets displace internal organs, don't you?" Momma was saying. "And interfere with digestion? And—"

"I know all that and I don't care!" Rose crossed her arms in front of her chest and looked pointedly at the door. "I have to get dressed for school."

Momma hesitated with her hand on the doorknob. "I don't want to bother you, but do you want me to help you find something, Rose? With everything still packed away . . ."

It wasn't like Momma to look so uncertain and Rose's heart softened.

"It's important to look *right* in a new school, and I have no idea what that would be," Rose said. She wasn't even good at looking right at Miss Dalyrumple's. Fashions seemed to come and go so fast, and Rose was always behind the leaders in her class. "What do they wear in New England, anyway?"

"My guess is the girls here might dress more simply," Mother said.

"I just want to blend in," Rose said. She frowned at herself in the mirror. Her white corset had blue ribbon to match the ribbon threaded through her pretty eyelet petticoat. But her collarbones stuck out and her face was too angular. "I'm not a Gibson girl, that's for sure."

"Rose, she's just a product of Charles Dana Gibson's imagination. I'm not saying he's not a good artist, but she's not real. No one looks like the Gibson girl."

You do, Rose thought.

"I know she's not real," Rose said, "but she's on plates and calendars and there's all that Gibson girl fashion because everyone loves her type. And look at me!"

"Oh Rosie! You need time to grow into yourself. And sweetie—you *are* beautiful."

"I know, 'inner beauty.'" Rose sighed. "I hate being new and not knowing a soul and . . . "

Mother stroked Rose's long black hair. "It's awfully hard, but it can be a great adventure, too. I know you'll miss the friends you left behind, but you'll meet new people."

I have no friends to miss, Rose thought.

"Remember how you loved Cape Light when we were here on vacation?" Momma smiled. "We could hardly drag you home."

Because of Summer Glory, Rose thought. She smiled back, remembering. When they had visited Aunt Norma and Uncle Ned, Rose had spent every minute at their stables. Glory was the most beautiful palomino, with a shining golden coat, a white mane, and a white tail. Glory had been sold two years ago, to a good home, Uncle Ned had promised. Rose remembered every detail: white patches on her face and on her legs below the knees, a muzzle like velvet, the soft nickering. If Uncle Ned had known then that the Forbes would move to Cape Light, maybe he would have saved Summer Glory for her. She was so sweet and friendly. . . .

Momma broke into the bittersweet memory. "Come, let's find something for you to wear."

Most of Rose's clothes were still packed in the big trunk in the center of her new bedroom. She opened the creaky lid and the lavender fragrance of their Gramercy Park apartment drifted into the air. The house on Lighthouse Lane had smelled musty when they arrived yesterday. They'd opened all the windows for the March wind to air it out.

Mother looked into the trunk and smiled. "Look, your scrapbooks, right on top."

Rose nodded and touched her precious horse scrapbooks, her wish books. The pages contained the treasured items she'd cut out or sent away for: feed catalogs, tack brochures, horse-grooming supplies, instructional sheets, how to plait a mane, newspaper clippings, and pictures of horses, mostly palominos. One scrapbook was filled and bulging, the second one was well under way.

"You can go to Uncle Ned's stables after school today." Momma knew exactly what to say to sweeten the move, Rose thought.

Rose dug through the clothes at the top of the trunk and found her sky-blue cotton shirtwaist and blue plaid wool skirt.

"What do you think, Momma?"

"You can't go wrong on the side of simplicity."

"With my black high-button shoes?"

Mother nodded. "Your shoes are still in the boxes downstairs. I'll find them for you. And I'd better get breakfast started. My goodness, I'll have to find a cook and a cleaning girl. Do you want hotcakes?"

"No, nothing. I can't eat a thing."

"At least a bite, Rose." Momma left the room with a swish of skirt and rustling petticoats, trailing lily of the valley perfume. She had to be turning over a new leaf, Rose thought. Hopefully she'd only wear *skirts* in Cape Light.

Rose put the shirtwaist on over her corset. It was simple, but ruffles and bows might be too fancy for a one-room school. She couldn't imagine what the William McKinley School would be like, with all different grades jammed in together. Would she have anyone to play with at recess, or would she be all alone again, off on the side and pretending not to mind?

Rose swallowed the big lump in her throat. Her fingers felt stiff with fear as she maneuvered the little pearl buttons on her dress through the holes.

Cape Light is my chance for a fresh start, Rose thought as she went down the stairs, her hand trailing along the mahogany banister. Please, God, maybe Momma has learned her lesson. Please let her do nothing here but be charming. It's her chance to start fresh, too. I so want to *honor* my mother, the way Your commandment says, and not be ashamed of her.

"Good morning, Poppa." The downstairs of the house was still cluttered with boxes and packing supplies; she had to pick her way around them in the dining room.

"Good morning, Rose." Poppa was in shirtsleeves; his salt-and-pepper mustache and beard looked uncombed. He was pushing a wooden crate down the hall. "All ready for school?"

"Yes, except for my shoes." Rose wondered if Momma had found them yet. She raised the lid of one of the boxes. Oh no! It was filled with pamphlets—suffragette literature!

"I thought she'd left all that behind! She *can't* pass this out in a new town!" Rose's eyes were wide with horror. "*Please* tell me she won't."

Poppa only shrugged.

A rush of anger left two bright spots in her cheeks. "Poppa, why aren't you upset? All the gossip about Momma made you give up your practice!"

"It might be a blessing, Rose. I'm truly *needed* here. The nearest doctor is over in Cranberry and, especially now, with scarlet fever spreading up and down the coast . . ." He smiled. "Of course, I might be paid in fish instead of cash."

"Momma!" Rose called.

Momma appeared in the doorway. "I haven't found the shoe crate yet, I'm still looking."

"What is this—this literature doing here? Tell me this was sent along by accident!" Rose waved a pamphlet in her hand. "We were all going to make a fresh start, weren't we?"

"Rose, it's such a wonderful opportunity," Momma said. "The movement needs grassroots demonstrations in places *exactly* like Cape Light. Every year the amendment is defeated by Congress and we have to show the politicians that women will fight for it, women in small towns just like this." Momma smiled. "You know, I think I wound up here in Cape Light for a purpose: to spread the message."

"Please, Momma. You can't!"

Momma's eyes flashed. "I most certainly can!"

What was she going to do about Momma? It was starting all over again. . . .

⇜*two*⇝

"Class, this is Rose Forbes," Miss Cotter, the teacher, announced. "I hope you'll make her feel welcome."

At the front of the room, Rose tried to smile. So many eyes were staring at her! There had to be close to sixty children, boys and girls of all ages and sizes. Some were smiling back at her, and others looked her over curiously.

"Joanna, please show Rose around and tell her where everything is. See me later, Rose, and we'll check where you belong in arithmetic and spelling." Miss Cotter sighed and tucked a few stray brown hairs back into her bun. She seemed a bit harried, but nice enough. She wore a white apron pinned to her black dress; Rose supposed that was to keep the chalk off her clothing. The assistant teacher, Miss Harding, was younger but she had a sour old-maid look.

Joanna jumped up from her desk and walked Rose around the crowded room. Her buckteeth made her look like an over-eager rabbit. Through her confusion, Rose tried to take in everything that Joanna pointed out. "The cubbyholes . . . and over there for coats and boots . . . that's the sewing table and . . ." Joanna drew Rose to the back window. "See over there? That's the outhouse."

Rose swallowed hard as she looked at the small wooden structure. An outhouse! Like in the slums of the lower east side of Manhattan! Did Poppa know about this? He'd had their house remodeled for indoor plumbing before they moved in. Miss Dalyrumple's and the apartment on Gramercy Park had had indoor bathrooms for ages!

"The boys will tell you there's snakes in there, but they're lying so don't believe them," Joanna went on. "Now if you need more ink in your inkwell . . . in this cabinet . . ."

Joanna led her around the classroom. Rose couldn't make sense of the way the students were grouped. A girl with long, tangled red hair was working with crayons at a table with the littlest children—and she *had* to be around Rose's age!

Joanna followed her glance. "Oh, that's Kat Williams.

She's awfully good at drawing, so she teaches the art projects." Joanna lowered her voice. "Kat's a daredevil and is always getting in trouble. Last fall, she stowed away on a fishing boat. It sank and they all had to be rescued!"

The redhead had a big smile for the little children. She looked cheerful and not especially troublesome to Rose.

"You moved into old Mr. Reynolds's house on Lighthouse Lane yesterday afternoon, didn't you?" Joanna said.

"Yes. How do you know that?" Rose asked.

"Oh, everybody's heard all about you. Your father's a doctor and you came from New York City and your mother's sister is Mrs. Clayton from Clayton Stables." Joanna stopped for a breath.

"That's my aunt Norma." A shiver ran through Rose. Cape Light was a small town where everyone knew all about everyone else! What if someone found out about Momma's arrest?

"Anyway, Kat lives on Lighthouse Lane, too," Joanna continued. "She lives in the lighthouse all the way at the very end at Durham Point."

"*In* the lighthouse?" Rose asked.

"Well, in the cottage right next to it. Her father's the lighthouse keeper. See that dark-haired boy over there?"

Rose followed Joanna's gesture to a thin, shabbily dressed boy.

"That's Robert. Watch out for him, he's mean. He likes to dip girls' braids into the inkwells. Some people say you have to forgive him 'cause his pa was lost when the *Silver Gull* sank last year. Over there, two seats away, that's Grace—she's my best friend. Did you meet Amanda Morgan yet?"

"No," Rose said. Joanna was pointing at a very pretty girl with light brown hair across the room.

"Oh, I thought you might have, because Amanda lives right across from you on Lighthouse Lane, on the ocean side. She's the minister's daughter. Amanda's nice, but she can never play or do anything because she has to take care of her little sister—that's Hannah at the spelling table, she's six—'cause their mother died when Hannah was born." Joanna talked very fast and spit a little as she spoke. Rose was careful to stay out of range. "Amanda is pals with Kat and that's odd 'cause they're nothing alike. So . . . I guess I've showed you everything."

"Yes, thank you."

"Let's go sit at my desk."

They crossed the room and Rose thought, I could have worn almost anything today and still fit in. One girl wore a threadbare dress. Its flowered print was faded colorless from too many washings. Kat, the redhead, wore a simple brown calico dress and pinafore. And then there was a blond girl flouncing over to the cabinet, her pink silk dress looking as elegant as anything you'd see at Miss Dalyrumple's, with deep ruffles at the hem and at the end of the sleeves. The bodice had embroidery in a darker pink and her high-button suede shoes matched exactly.

"That blond girl you're looking at? That's Lizabeth Merchant," Joanna said. "Lizabeth is Kat's cousin. Did you see the big, fancy white house on Lighthouse Lane right near the village green—the one with the front porch and the arches and the rose trellis?"

Rose shook her head. "I haven't been here long enough to see anything."

"Well, that's Lizabeth's house. Her father runs the bank and all, but honestly, Lizabeth thinks she's *royalty!*" Joanna wrinkled her nose. "She thinks far too much of herself, if you ask me."

Joanna prattled on and on, about Gwendolyn, and about Mark, the blacksmith's son. She's friendly, Rose thought, but she's an awful gossip—and that's dangerous!

If she ever learned about Momma . . . Rose wanted a friend badly, but she decided to steer clear of Joanna.

Miss Cotter noticed that Joanna was still talking and said, "That's quite enough, Joanna. Get started on your reader. And Rose, please come here."

Miss Cotter checked Rose's reading, spelling, and arithmetic. Rose was well ahead of her age group in reading and spelling, but a little behind in arithmetic. That surprised her. She'd thought Miss Dalyrumple's students would be ahead in everything. While Miss Cotter talked about catching up, Rose looked around the class for girls her age. Would anyone but Joanna talk to her? Maybe she could manage to gather her courage and approach someone at recess . . . maybe Amanda Morgan, since she lived across the street.

But Rose didn't have to gather her courage at all. When they were released by Miss Cotter's bell, Kat, Amanda, and Lizabeth rushed over to her in the schoolyard, with Kat in the lead.

Kat had a big, brilliant smile. "I couldn't wait to talk to you! I've always wanted to meet someone from New York City!"

"Kat wants to be an artist in a big city," Amanda explained.

"Someday," Kat said, "though I love Cape Light. But I'm dying to know what it's like to live in New York. What were your very favorite things?"

Kat bubbled over with high spirits—no shy pauses in her conversation!

Rose took a minute to gather her thoughts. "Well, I liked seeing vaudeville," she said, "especially at Proctor's. It had the biggest stars. Weber and Fields, Eva Tanguay, and the Three Keatons."

"Go on," Kat prompted.

"I saw Harry Houdini escape from a straitjacket once. Even my father couldn't figure out how he did it."

Kat looked so interested that Rose was encouraged to continue. "And Coney Island is exciting. Luna Park has Ferris wheels and roller coasters and millions of electric lightbulbs that make you think a summer night has turned into daytime!"

"I'll see that someday." Kat's eyes were shining. "What else?"

"I like Central Park. It has bridle paths and . . . I take riding lessons and—"

"Is the park big enough to ride in?" Amanda looked puzzled.

"Central Park is *huge*. Over eight hundred acres.

With a lake where you can go rowing and even a meadow where sheep graze."

"Sheep? You mean there's a farm in the middle of the park?" Lizabeth asked.

"No, they're just for show. For atmosphere," Rose said. "What about Cape Light? What does everyone do here?"

"I guess it's kind of sleepy compared to New York City," Kat said. "I like outdoor things best. I love skating in the winter when the pond freezes over. And I go clamming, and there's a waterhole we swim in, though the water is always cold. We can't go into the ocean. There's an undertow and the shoreline is all rocks."

"Sometimes there are hayrides and that's so much fun," Amanda said. "And last year we had a barn dance. That was after the barn raising when lightning hit the Hallorans'."

Nearby, some of the boys were playing snap the whip. At the other end of the yard, girls were lined up to jump rope. Kat, Lizabeth, and Amanda seemed content to spend recess talking to her, Rose thought, and talking with them came easily.

Her happiness was spoiled a little when Lizabeth said, "I can't wait to see how you're redecorating Mr.

Reynolds's old house."

"Well . . . we're not anywhere near settled in yet," Rose said. She'd *never* bring anyone home again! There was no telling what Momma might be up to! "It . . . it might take us quite a while."

Amanda nodded sympathetically. She was easily the prettiest girl at William McKinley, Rose thought, not dramatic like Momma with her striking coloring, but in a quiet way, with light brown hair and long-lashed hazel eyes. Rose liked her soft-spoken manner.

Miss Cotter rang the bell marking the end of recess. On the way back inside, Rose fought against her shyness and asked Amanda, "Want to walk home together after school? Since we live right across the lane from each other?"

"I would, any other day." Amanda gave a sweet smile. "But my little sister is playing at Mary Margaret's after school, so I'm free to go to the lighthouse today."

"Oh." Rose scrunched her shoulders together.

She caught Amanda's quick glance at Kat and Kat's nod.

"Why don't you come with us?" Amanda said.

"Lizabeth is coming over, too," Kat said. "The lighthouse tower is our special place. Well, you'll see."

"Thank you, but . . . I don't know," Rose said. She had been planning to stop at home after school just long enough to pick up her riding hat and boots and then go straight to Uncle Ned's stables. She had so looked forward to that! She couldn't wait one more day . . . or could she? "I don't think I . . . that's so nice of you."

Lizabeth grinned. "We're not being nice. We're just thrilled to see a new face in town. We get quite bored with each other."

"No, we don't!" Amanda protested.

"Girls, stop dallying!" Miss Cotter called. "Back to class!"

"Immediately!" Miss Harding added.

"Come over, Rose," Kat said as they scurried back into the schoolroom. "Well, unless you have something important to do."

"All right," Rose said breathlessly. "Thank you!" It wasn't as though Summer Glory was still there, whinnying for her at the gate. She could manage to wait one more day to see the horses because, after the long spell of loneliness, she had three new friends!

three

Rose, Kat, Lizabeth, and Amanda walked from school along William McKinley Road. Once in a while, Kat darted ahead as though she couldn't contain her energy and then doubled back, her belted books swinging in wide arcs.

They turned right at Lighthouse Lane. "My house is the other way, where the lane is civilized and *paved*," Lizabeth told Rose, waving her arm toward the village green. They had reached the section of Lighthouse Lane where it became a rocky road and curved toward the ocean.

They passed Rose's house and Lizabeth admired the twin gas-lamps out front. Amanda's cottage across the street was nestled among tall trees and overlooked the shore.

"The lighthouse isn't that far from here," Kat told Rose.

"Yes it is," Lizabeth said. "It's half a mile. If Lighthouse Lane was paved all the way, we could ride our bicycles."

"Do you all have bicycles?" Rose asked.

"I don't yet. I'm saving for one," Kat said.

"In the city, there are trolleys and horse-drawn carriages you can hail," Rose said. "I guess I'll need a bicycle here."

"We still walk mostly everywhere," Amanda said. "Nothing is that far away. Lighthouse Lane is the longest road. It goes from one end of Cape Light to the other."

Farther from the village green, the houses became smaller. Fish netting was spread to dry along the width of one front porch. Rose noticed whalebone decorations on some of the lawns.

They came to the long, steep hill where Lighthouse Lane led down to the shore. Here the lane was lined by beach plum and sea grass. They passed Wharf Way, the busy docks, the bait-and-tackle shed, and Alveria & Sons Boatyard.

I can't believe I'm going to live in a fishing village, Rose thought. Along with the smell of fish, Rose was picking up a clean, salty scent. Yellow buds of forsythia poked out on branches among the brush.

In the distance, Rose saw the lighthouse tower rising high above its surroundings. The glass windows at the top glistened in the sun. She had the strangest feeling that it was beckoning to her.

They arrived at Kat's cottage. Rose was surprised by how humble it was. It had a rough stone floor and one big room that served as the kitchen, dining room, and living room. The girls, Kat's two younger brothers, Todd and James, and a big white dog named Sunshine crowded together in a noisy group. Mrs. Williams was the quiet center of it all.

There was something so welcoming about Kat's mother. It wasn't only the way she said, "I hope you'll love Cape Light, Rose." It was the warmth of her smile, the crinkles around her kind blue eyes, and the way she lightly touched Rose's shoulder.

Mrs. Williams served oatmeal cookies, still warm from the oven. Her work-worn hands looked strong and competent. "This has to be a big change from New York City," she said. "No one even locks their doors in Cape Light. I was just reading in yesterday's newspaper about all the turmoil going on in Manhattan. There was a convention of those women agitating for the vote—"

"Suffragettes," Kat put in.

"Yes," Mrs. Williams continued, "and there was a near riot." She looked at Rose. "Had you heard much about that?"

"I haven't kept up with the news," Rose said. That was true, but she had an awful feeling, as though she were lying.

"Women shouldn't be concerned with politics; that goes against the natural order of things," Mrs. Williams said. "It's quite enough that Mr. Williams's vote represents his family."

The few boys Rose knew didn't seem any wiser or more capable of choosing a president than she was. But maybe it was different when they were grown up.

"And to actually demonstrate and disrupt traffic," Mrs. Williams went on. "Well, those women are troublemakers."

Though Momma's activities embarrassed Rose, she'd never thought they were truly *wrong*. She liked and respected Mrs. Williams. She didn't know what to think now.

"If I lived in Boston or New York," Kat said, "I'd be a suffragette in a minute."

Mrs. Williams shook her head. "You don't mean that."

"You know Kat, Aunt Jean," Lizabeth said. "She always has to be contrary."

Rose was relieved when Todd changed the subject to talk about his report on Eskimos and igloos.

"Has everyone finished?" Kat asked. "Let's go to the tower."

Rose followed the other girls as they hurried along the short path to the lighthouse. Rose couldn't shake the uncanny feeling that she was *meant* to be there. And that somehow she was coming back to a place where she had been before—though she knew she hadn't! She had certainly never climbed up a long ladder in a narrow dark shaft surrounded by curved stone walls. When she finally reached the tower at the top of the ladder, she was blinded by the sunlight flooding into the round room. Huge windows curved all around.

Rose caught her breath. Below, the ocean stretched as far as she could see. The steady beat of the waves lapping at the shore was hypnotic. With miles of sky all around, the tower seemed to float above the clouds.

"Well, what do you think?" Kat watched her, grinning.

"It *is* a special place," Rose whispered.

"Our place. The tower is really for standing watch

after dark," Kat said, "to make sure that the light is on and rotating and that no ships are in trouble. That's my family's job."

"But Kat, Amanda, and I—we meet here whenever we can," Lizabeth said.

Rose spotted some watercolor paintings propped up on a shelf. They were amazing depictions of the scene from the windows. "These are wonderful. Where did you get them?"

"Kat painted them," Lizabeth said.

Rose looked at Kat in surprise. "I thought . . . I thought a professional artist had come up here. I can't believe how good they are!"

"Thank you." Kat smiled, coloring with pleasure.

"Kat dreams about being a famous artist," Amanda said.

Kat shook her head. "Not famous, so much. A *good* artist."

"Come on, Kat, admit it," Lizabeth said. "You intend to be *great*. The greatest artist who ever lived, woman or not!"

"Lizabeth dreams about silk and satin and the latest fashions from France," Kat said.

"I think about other things, too," Lizabeth protested.

"Oops, sorry," Kat said. "I left out lace and feathered hats and—"

"Oh, stop!" Lizabeth laughed.

It was mild, affectionate teasing, Rose thought, that showed what very good friends they were. They were lucky.

Kat smiled. "And Amanda dreams about a certain boy—"

"Who stares at her in church," Lizabeth continued.

Amanda stood up and went to a window, quickly turning her back to them. "Let's do something. Play jacks or—"

"She doesn't want us to see her blush." Lizabeth giggled. "In fact, ever since the barn dance, they're madly in love!"

Amanda whirled around. "I'm not in love! I'm much too young to even *think* of courting!"

Rose could see that the teasing was bothering Amanda. Don't they see the sadness in her eyes, Rose wondered. But Lizabeth continued with, "Well, Jed Langford certainly thinks of . . . "

Impulsively Rose interrupted to deflect their attention. "*I'm* the one who's in love," she announced.

"You are?" Amanda asked. "Do your parents know?"

"With someone in New York?" Kat asked.

"Tell us!" Lizabeth's eyes were wide. "With who?"

Rose laughed. "With horses!"

"Oh, please." Lizabeth groaned.

"No, really," Rose said. "It happened here at Clayton Stables, when I was ten. I just fell for them. I wasn't the least bit afraid. I just loved their soft muzzles, and the way their ears and nostrils flutter, and their whinnies. And the flowing manes, and the large eyes with those lovely lashes. When we came back to the city, I kept dreaming of the smell of the stables: the hay, the molasses feed—"

Lizabeth rolled her eyes. "And the manure."

"Even that. I just wanted to be there."

Kat smiled. "You really did fall in love."

"I started riding lessons as soon as I came home. And now for the best thing! Uncle Ned promised I could pick a horse, one special horse for me to ride!" Rose couldn't keep the excitement out of her voice.

"But if you rode in the city, isn't that the same thing?" Amanda asked.

"Oh, no, not at all! At riding class I had a different horse every time. There's no chance to really get to know one. It's like renting a dog for an hour! Those horses have to put up with riders who yank too hard on their reins and hurt their mouths, and riders who don't know how to post and bounce on their backs. The horses just want to get back to their stalls." Rose sighed. "It was the only place I could take lessons. I was learning to jump. I love that! And I *needed* to learn, so someday when I have a horse of my own . . ."

Rose bit her lip. She had been going on and on. "I'm sorry. Honestly, I never talk this much."

Amanda smiled. "When we're in the tower, we all talk a lot."

"So your dream is to have a horse of your own," Kat said, "and now it's about to come true."

"It won't *really* be my own horse," Rose corrected. "Uncle Ned might still use it for riding classes or for breeding, but I'll have the same horse to ride every time, and we'll get to know each other and I'll ride every single day and . . . It's almost as good as having my own."

"When can you pick it?" Lizabeth asked.

"Anytime. I can't wait! I was going to the stables right after school, but then you invited me here and—"

"Well, the afternoon's not over and I want to see you choose," Kat said.

"Let's all go," Amanda said.

"Riding clothes are elegant," Lizabeth said. "I love the scarlet jackets and black velvet hats they wear for fox hunting."

Kat stared at her. "Who'd want to hunt a poor little fox?"

"I saw it in a magazine," Lizabeth said. "They have hunt breakfasts and wear the most elegant clothes."

"My mother bought a divided skirt for me so I don't have to ride sidesaddle," Rose said. "It's a brand-new fashion that was introduced in Saratoga. You know, where the famous racetrack is in upstate New York."

Amanda looked shocked. "Does it look like wearing *trousers*?"

"No, it's wide and flared, mostly like a skirt, I guess. It's much easier to keep your balance astride."

"*Astride?*" Lizabeth said. "You mean with your legs parted? Like a man?"

"Just so you can use your legs to direct the horse," Rose said.

"And a divided skirt is all right with your *mother*?" Lizabeth asked. "She actually *gave* it to you?"

Rose wished she had never mentioned it. Maybe it was acceptable for riding class in New York, but it would never do in Cape Light! What had she been thinking? "My mother was just . . . just showing me what funny things they wear in Saratoga. It was a joke."

"It makes sense for riding," Kat said, "or biking—you could ride a *boy's* bike—or if you need to climb a tree."

"Why would you ever need to climb a tree?" Lizabeth asked.

"For the fun of it! I'd love a skirt like that," Kat said.

Kat's not quiet and inside herself like I am, Rose thought. She'll say *anything*!

"Should we stop off at your house and get it before we—" Kat started.

"Oh, no," Rose said quickly. There was no telling what Momma might be up to! "I won't even stop for my boots and hat. I . . . I guess I won't ride today, I'll just . . . Let's just go straight to my uncle Ned's and choose a horse!"

$\mathscr{e}$ *four* $\mathscr{e}$

The smell of hay and the deep, moist breaths of the horses filled Rose's heart.

"Now Monogram here . . . I admit he's not much to look at. His back is a little swayed and he's a little cow-hocked." Uncle Ned had led Rose, Amanda, Lizabeth, and Kat past a row of stalls.

They had reached the last stall and they were looking at a plain brown horse, about sixteen hands high. Rose listened closely to Uncle Ned's every word.

"But Monogram is a nice horse, easy to get along with, and a pleasure around the barn. Intelligent, always willing—"

Monogram interrupted by leaning his head over the stall door and nuzzling Uncle Ned's shoulder. Uncle Ned smiled and patted the massive muzzle. "A lot of heart in this horse, Rose."

The girls trailed Uncle Ned outdoors from the stable

and along the path leading to the paddocks. In the sunlight, Uncle Ned's deeply tanned skin looked leathery, with deep crinkles around his eyes. His light brown hair had sun-bleached streaks.

He pointed to a corral in the far distance. "Yonder are the broodmares due to foal later this spring. You'll want to see the colts."

Colts! And horses, horses, horses. This was heaven. Rose was sure the air smelled sweeter here and the sky was bluer.

"Have you seen one you like yet?" Uncle Ned asked her.

"I like them all!"

The near paddock had horses of all sizes and colors. Some grazed peacefully, moving slowly to new tufts of grass. Some stood at rest in the shade of a tree. Others frolicked together, kicking up their back legs. It made Rose's heart sing to see horses being—well, just being natural horses. She was sure they were enjoying this soft early spring day.

When they approached the paddock, Rose's attention was drawn by a sudden burst of movement. A dark horse galloped away to the fence on the far side of the paddock.

Rose was riveted. He was a beauty, dark chestnut

with a moon-shaped white marking between his eyes. His flowing mane and tail were inky black. His legs were slender, etched and muscular. He stood still as a statue, shining in the sunlight, a breathtaking picture against the green of the grass and the white post-and-rail fence.

"That horse," Rose breathed. "The chestnut."

"Midnight Star," Uncle Ned said. "Beautiful, isn't he? I'm selling him next week."

Uncle Ned pointed. "The Appaloosa there is American Eagle, a ten-year-old gelding. Very spirited, but a little immature."

Rose couldn't take her eyes from the chestnut horse. Did Uncle Ned mean Midnight Star had already been promised to a buyer? She was suddenly heartsick.

"Eagle doesn't get scared, but he gets confused and he'll stop cold," Uncle Ned was saying. Rose forced herself to pay attention. "You have to find a way to make things clear to him."

Star's silky black mane . . . Rose imagined burying her face in it as she rode. . . .

"Nellie is the little dappled mare under the tree," Uncle Ned continued. "Now she's a sweetheart. Obedient and gentle. She tends to shy sometimes, but it's nothing you can't handle."

Rose wrenched her eyes from Star to look at the mare.

"I'd pick Nellie," Amanda said.

"I'd take American Eagle," Kat said, "or that spirited one we saw back in the stalls. Clayton's Comet."

"You can take your time and see which horse you get along with best, Rose." Uncle Ned's eyes swept her from head to shoes. "Though I won't let you ride without boots and a hard hat, you know that."

"I'll bring them tomorrow," Rose mumbled.

As they reached the fence, American Eagle whinnied and trotted toward them. "Hoping for a carrot." Uncle Ned smiled. "That horse has no manners."

Maybe Star wasn't *definitely* promised to someone else, Rose thought.

"Now next to Nellie, that's Toby Boy with the white stockings, part Arabian and a little rambunctious, but—"

"Wait, Uncle Ned, tell me about Midnight Star," Rose interrupted.

"Star? He's a five-year-old thoroughbred, bred to race."

"Has someone already bought him?" Please say no, Rose thought.

"No."

"Oh, I'm so glad, Uncle Ned!" She wanted to jump and dance and whirl around. "I choose Midnight Star!"

"No, Rose. He's not the right horse for you."

"But why not?" Rose asked. "I don't understand."

"Take my word for it. Forget him."

"But . . . why?"

"From what I understand, he was pushed into racing too early, before his joints had developed properly." Uncle Ned boosted himself up and sat on the top rail of the fence. "Star was fast and as long as he won, no one especially cared if his training caused him suffering."

"Suffering?" Amanda whispered.

An uncomfortable tingle started in the small of Rose's back.

"He had a strained tendon—that's when they say a horse is broke down—and maybe they cold-hosed it to lessen the swelling and worked him again too soon. He was still a moneymaker. Though I heard they had a devil of a time forcing Star into the gate."

Rose dreaded hearing more. She wanted to close her ears and her mind from whatever else was coming. But she couldn't turn away.

"He won a fair number of races for a while," Uncle Ned continued, "but then—my guess is he couldn't handle the pain anymore—he started losing. If you touch his flanks, you can feel the scars from the whip."

Rose winced.

"Pretty good records are kept on racehorses. But after he was sold off, that's where I lose the trail. No telling how many times he changed hands. By the time I saw him, he was skin and bones; someone had half-starved him."

Rose couldn't help picturing him with protruding ribs, bones jutting through the unkempt chestnut hide, the stomach caved in with aching hunger. Oh, Star!

"I was at a horse fair downstate and he was in a group with some old, lame carriage horses, bought up for slaughter. A sad thing to see. And you know, there was something about Star in the middle of that group—class in his conformation, some kind of dignity—that made me go ahead and buy him from the slaughterer. A foolish impulse, I guess. I was betting that with quality feed and plenty of rest out in the field, he might be all right."

"He is! He looks wonderful now, Uncle Ned." There was a happy ending to Star's story!

"He does, Mr. Clayton," Kat added.

"He's not all right," Uncle Ned said. "It's nothing physical beyond what you'd expect in an ex-racehorse. But this horse was bullied. His experience with people was all about fear and abuse. Did you see how he galloped as far from us as he could get when we approached the fence? He won't bolt outright—my guess is that's brought him painful punishment before—but he's always anxious and on the verge of rearing, expecting the worst from you. He's paralyzed with tension. I can't use him for riding instruction, he's a gelding so he's no good for breeding, and . . . I have to get rid of him. I have someone coming for him next week."

"What does that mean?" Rose's voice broke. "Does that mean he'll be sold for slaughter?"

"Could be." Uncle Ned looked uncomfortable. "Look, I don't like it, but what am I supposed to do with him? I tried. I saved him once. But nobody can reach him. I can't palm him off on someone for pleasure riding."

"After all he's been through, Mr. Clayton," Kat said, "couldn't he just stay here?"

"I'm as sorry as anybody. But caring for a horse properly is expensive—the feed is the least of it. There's the grooming—I have to tell you, the grooms don't like dealing with his hostility—the shoes, worming, even the stall space. I board horses, too, and I have only so many stablehands. I'm sorry, but each horse here has to earn its keep or Clayton Stables fails." Uncle Ned hopped off the fence rail and took a step forward on the path. "Come, I want to show you Cheyenne Princess."

Kat, Amanda, and Lizabeth started to follow along, but Rose couldn't move.

"Star is the one I want, Uncle Ned."

"Rose, take a look at Princess. She has a kind eye and—"

"Star is the only one I want."

Uncle Ned looked at her, puzzled. "Why would you pick a horse like that over Nellie or Eagle?"

"Why would you?" Lizabeth echoed.

Star stood still and wary, far off in the field.

"Because I have to save him," Rose said.

Rose *knew* she couldn't possibly see Star's eyes from this distance, so how could she think he was looking directly at her? But he was! She felt it.

Rose had always liked Uncle Ned. She was dismayed to think that he might be heartless.

"If Star is difficult because he was abused," Rose said, "are you going to punish him for that by letting him be slaughtered? For . . . for glue or dog food? That's wrong!"   .

Uncle Ned met her beseeching stare. "I'm running a business."

"It's still wrong." Rose locked her eyes into his.

Uncle Ned looked both annoyed and defensive. "It would be very nice to run a rescue operation for abused and abandoned horses. That takes funding. Do you have the funding, Rose?"

Rose forced herself to keep from looking away. She *wouldn't* let herself be intimidated by his sarcasm! But she softened her tone. "Please let me try to turn him around. Please, Uncle Ned, give me some time with him."

Uncle Ned dropped his gaze first. "You'll change your mind when you get a closer look," he said. "Let's lead him in."

The girls waited while Uncle Ned picked up a bridle and reins. Then they went into the paddock and across the grass.

As they came closer to Star, Rose could see how stiffly he held himself.

"Stay away from his back legs, you never know," Uncle Ned told the girls. "Fear could make him dangerous."

The horse made no attempt to kick or run, but he seemed to be shrinking from them.

"Do you want to put the bridle on?" Uncle Ned asked Rose.

She nodded.

"Always work from his left side," he said.

"I know."

Star, motionless, allowed her to put the bridle in place and adjust the bit. Anyone watching, Rose thought, would think this was an easy horse to handle. But Rose felt the trembling and the tension in his body. She sensed his clamped-down quiet terror.

All horses' eyes are large and dark and set in the same place on their heads, Rose thought, but they're all completely different. Star's eyes weren't curious or out-going. His gaze was inward, as though he was trying to be far away from everything around him. Dear God, she thought, one of your most noble creatures has been hor-ribly damaged. Please, God, if there is any way to heal him, help me find it.

"Lead him back to the stalls," Uncle Ned told her.

With her right hand, Rose held both reins five inches below the bit, under Star's chin, as she had been taught.

"Come on now," she said softly, "you're fine, Star."

There was no response to her voice. It may be love at first sight for me, Rose thought, but certainly not for him. When she gave the reins a gentle tug and walked forward at his side, the horse followed, but it was clear that each step was unwilling.

"I know, Star, I understand," Rose murmured. "I know."

She led Star to the stall that Uncle Ned indicated. She was careful to open the door all the way and she pushed aside the latch so that nothing would jab Star in the side.

Once in the stall, the horse hugged the far wall, as far from her as a large body in a small space would allow.

"You see what I mean?" Uncle Ned said. "He hates people."

"Do you blame him?" Rose asked.

"You won't have a relationship with him," Uncle Ned said. "Not a moment's pleasure. It won't be like Summer Glory."

"He *is* beautiful," Lizabeth said, "but Nellie's pretty, so why don't you—"

"Because Nellie doesn't need me," Rose said. "I can't let him go. Please, Uncle Ned."

She felt Kat's sympathetic hand on her shoulder.

"Your stablehands won't have to do a thing. I'll take care of him, Uncle Ned. I'll groom him myself, I know how, and—"

"And muck out the stall and bring in fresh hay and water? That's a day in, day out job and you'll be busy with school."

"I'll do it, Uncle Ned."

"How can you?" he asked.

"I'll help her," Kat said. "I promise I will."

"So will I, whenever I can," Amanda said.

After a pause, Lizabeth said, "Me, too. I don't know about actually mucking out a stall, but I'll do something."

Uncle Ned scratched his head.

"I promise I'll keep up with my schoolwork." Rose stood rigid, both hopeful and worried. "I'll do everything I'm supposed to do." She watched his every breath. "Please give Star a chance."

"All right, here's what I'll do," Uncle Ned finally said. "I'll wait until the horse show in North Menasha. That's on April twenty-eighth. All kinds of buyers come to the auction there. Maybe Star can get into a better situation if you can manage to make him friendlier."

It was March nineteenth—that gave her six weeks. "Thank you, Uncle Ned!"

"Don't count on it, Rose. I think Midnight Star will break your heart."

~*five*~

The four girls walked from Clayton Stables toward Lighthouse Lane along a curving, down-hill road. Most of Cape Light was a thin finger of land jutting into the sea, but here, west of the village square, the town widened.

They went by barns and freshly green pastures. They passed a horse pulling a plow through a field. The brown-black furrows behind him had a rich earthy smell. At Potter's Orchard, rows and rows of apple trees were budding with delicate new leaves of the softest green.

"Look at that! It makes me want to get my water-colors," Kat said. "Maybe I'll make paper with a border of pale spring leaves."

"Kat paints beautiful gift paper," Lizabeth explained. "It's sold at the general store and the book-shop on Pelican Street."

"And at the bakery," Kat added. "I like doing it

anyway, but I have to earn money to pay back Todd. He lent me five dollars when I really needed it and I still owe him two. He's the best brother anyone could have!"

"I wish I had brothers. Or sisters," Rose said.

"I wish *I* was an only child," Lizabeth said. "There's my sister, Tracy, who's a terrible pest and—"

"You don't mean that. She's only four and as cute as can be," Amanda put in.

"—and my brother, Christopher," Lizabeth went on. "He just turned fifteen. He goes to the high school in Cranberry and he thinks that makes him the boss of everybody!"

"Chris is nice when he's not being sarcastic," Kat said.

"Brothers and sisters." Lizabeth sighed. "Don't you get so tired of taking care of Hannah?"

"No," Amanda said. "It's the least I can do. Wait, I just had an idea! Hannah will be seven soon. That's old enough for riding, isn't it? If she takes a lesson at your uncle's one afternoon a week, it would be fun for her *and* I could be with all of you at the stables! I'll ask Father tonight."

"Maybe you'll want lessons, too," Rose said.

"Father keeps our horse and carriage at Hayward's

Livery Stable off the green," Amanda said, "I never even thought of riding before."

"Our horse and carriage are at the livery stable, too," Lizabeth said, "but that's different. They don't wear saddles." She looked at Rose. "Your father will probably use Hayward's, too. It's the closest to Lighthouse Lane."

Rose nodded. "I wish there was pasture for them near our houses."

"When Dobbins isn't pulling our wagon," Kat said, "he's mostly out in the field behind the chicken coop. Todd and I ride him bareback sometimes, but he goes pretty much wherever he wants to. And that's usually to the kitchen window for a handout from Ma."

The road joined Lighthouse Lane a few steps from Rose's and Amanda's homes. The girls paused for a moment, hesitant to separate; Lizabeth would go on toward the village square and Kat in the opposite direction toward the lighthouse.

Lizabeth looked at Rose's house. "I don't remember a side entrance there."

"That was put in before we moved. It's for my father's office and waiting room."

"Oh, so a lot has been done already," Lizabeth said.

Rose nodded uncomfortably. She knew Lizabeth

was curious to see the changes. But Rose could hear the syncopated piano, a clear sign that Momma was home.

Amanda heard it, too. "That music! Who's playing?"

Why did it have to be so loud, and why did Momma have to play ragtime—that bawdy dance-hall music! "My mother," Rose mumbled. Why didn't she play *"Für Elise"* like any normal mother would!

"She's good," Amanda said. "I love music and singing. I wish I could play the piano like that."

You don't wish you could play the "Maple Leaf Rag," Rose thought. That's completely inappropriate for the minister's daughter.

Rose twisted her fingers together. She was sure they expected to be invited in. They expected to be introduced to Momma. Any second, one of them would ask her, and what would she say then?

"I have to go," Rose said abruptly. "I'm late. I'm supposed to do something." Just before she whirled around to dash up her front path, she saw the startled expressions on their faces. They had to think she was terribly rude or peculiar or worse! She turned back at the door and called, "See you in school."

Kat nodded and Amanda half-waved, but they still had that puzzled look.

As soon as Rose opened the front door, the piano playing stopped with one last flourish and Momma came sashaying into the hall, working her way around crates of all sizes.

"There you are! Well, Rosie, how was your first day?"

"It was good. I made some new friends in school, I like them so much! And Momma, then I went to Uncle Ned's."

Momma smiled. "I thought so. Tell me the most important thing: Did you find a horse for yourself?"

"Yes, Momma. Midnight Star. He's a beautiful chestnut with a black mane." She wished she could think of him with an easy heart.

"Well, I hope your Midnight Star will be as lovable as Summer Glory. You had a wonderful day, didn't you?" Momma smiled that brilliant smile with all her dimples showing. "So did I!"

"You did?"

"Cape Light is the friendliest town. First, some women came by with a bunch of daffodils and a casserole to welcome us. Wasn't that nice? It's some kind of fish-and-potato dish. It doesn't sound that tasty to me, but it comes in handy for our supper tonight. And one of them, a Mrs. Merchant, said her cook Ada has a sister Edna who needs a position. So starting next week, we'll have a cook!"

Mrs. Merchant? Lizabeth's mother! Household help saw everything that was going on. What if Edna found out about Momma and talked to Ada? Then Lizabeth would know!

"That's not a good idea," Rose said. "I think you should go to an employment agency."

"There are no employment agencies in Cape Light," Momma said. "And a personal recommendation is always the best way. Why in the world would you think otherwise?"

Rose shrugged.

They made their way through the hall. "It'll take a while to get all these crates unpacked, but I'm working on it." Momma put her arm around Rose's shoulders and led her into the parlor. "This room will be lovely. I'll have that gloomy wallpaper removed, and paint the walls pale yellow. Oh, and one of the women invited me to come to the Ladies' Quilting Society this evening. It's a grand opportunity to meet more Cape Light women—though I can't quite imagine myself quilting, can you? Well, I'll try to learn how. There's a lot of artistry to it."

Momma's enthusiasm was contagious. She could make Rose believe that nothing but good things were in store for them. Rose knew she would turn this house into a delightful home, with pretty colors, and without the crowded jumble of ornaments and pictures that so many people favored.

"I'm sure you'll quilt beautifully if you put your mind to it," Rose said.

"Thank you, Rosie! Would you mind having supper now, so that I can get to the meeting in time? It seems people eat early and go to bed early here."

"That's fine. I'm hungry anyway. Where's Poppa?"

"He's still out on calls. He hasn't even had a chance to hang up his license in the office. It's as if Cape Light was holding its breath waiting for a doctor to move in. One broken arm . . ."

Rose followed Momma into the dining room and they set the shining mahogany table with monogrammed napkins and silverware.

". . . heart palpitations, a baby with croup, and a fainting spell. Sorry, I still can't find the tablecloths; I'll hunt for them tomorrow."

Soon they were sitting opposite each other with plates of fish-and-potato casserole. It was quite spicy and it tasted better than it sounded.

"I do wonder what people wear for quilting," Momma said. "I don't have the slightest idea. What do you think, Rosie?"

It wasn't like Momma to sound insecure about anything. Could even Momma be a tiny bit nervous about meeting new people?

"They'll love you, Momma, and you'll look beautiful no matter what you wear." Many times, Rose had seen people actually gasp at Momma's beauty. And they'd be entranced by her sparkle, by the lilt in her voice, and by her bubbling laughter. Sometimes Rose was so very proud of her, though it wasn't easy to be her quite unremarkable daughter. "But don't wear your bloomers!"

Momma raised her eyebrows. "I think I can judge when they're appropriate and when they're not."

"I just meant, they'll love you at the Quilting Society . . . if you don't say anything about suffragette things."

"I've told you, I prefer 'suffragist.' 'Suffragette' is another way of belittling us. And of course, I'm taking some pamphlets with me. It's a grand opportunity to pass them out."

Rose couldn't swallow another bite. "Momma, *please* don't. The quilting ladies will be dead set against the vote."

"Not all of them, Rose. Maybe some fear their husbands will be angry. Or that entering a polling place is 'unwomanly,' whatever that means! Or that if their hired girls get the vote, they would demand better pay and working conditions."

"Momma, you wouldn't talk to *Edna* about that if she comes to work for us!"

"I certainly would."

"Don't start that all over again, Momma. Not here!"

"I have to do what I think is right," Momma said.

"You don't give a thought to how it affects me and Father. You'll make me lose all my friends!"

"If you have real friends, nothing *I* do could matter."

"You think you can charm people all the time. You forget how quickly they turned on you. And the whole family! You offend people!"

Momma put her fork down. "It's far more offensive to have laws that don't allow me to vote or own property in my own name, or even be the legal guardian of my child."

Momma's lips were tight with anger, though her eyes looked wounded. She got up from the table. "Excuse me. I have to change for the meeting."

Rose watched Momma go upstairs. She could

picture her passing out pamphlets at the Quilting Society. What a nightmare! Momma had to be stopped! Did Momma do these things to get even more attention than her beauty commanded? Well, it was the *wrong* kind of attention!

Rose went into the hall and found the wooden box that contained the pamphlets. It was too heavy to lift. Rose could shove it a few inches across the floor. But then what? How could she get rid of it and where could she take it? She lifted the lid and looked at the top layer with distaste. WOMEN! STAND UP FOR YOUR RIGHTS NOW! The black block printing screamed from the page. In despair, Rose realized she had no plan and Momma would be on her way soon. And then an idea came to her: Hide it in plain sight!

In a frantic hurry, Rose opened the other crates and boxes to check their contents. Pots and pans—no. Poppa's books—no. Here were fluffy white bath towels. That would work. There was space between the pamphlets and the top of their box; Rose pressed the pamphlets down some more. Good, enough room to spread three bath towels on top. Rose closed the lid just as she heard Momma's footsteps on the stairs. She scampered back to her chair in the dining room.

It was horrible for Rose to sit still while Momma opened crate after crate. "You saw my pamphlets here this morning, didn't you, Rose? I know they were here somewhere."

"Yes, Momma." Rose got up to stand at the dining room door.

"Why can't I find them?" Momma opened *the* crate and Rose's heart skipped.

Momma glanced at the towels, and passed it by. She looked beautiful in a starched white shirtwaist with ruffled sleeves, but as she became more flustered, rushing to look in still more crates, her forehead became shiny with perspiration.

It was hard for Rose not to help her. "Momma, you'll be late. Why don't you forget about them for now?"

"It's just a matter of finding the right box." Her pretty shirtwaist was beginning to wilt. "I wanted to bring them with me *tonight*!" And, as she scraped her finger on another wooden lid, "Ow! A splinter!"

Rose was almost choking with guilt. "Do you want me to get it out for you? Let me help you."

Momma sucked her finger. "There's no time. I was late to begin with and now—" She looked distressed. "I suppose I'll have to bring the pamphlets another time."

"You'd better go, Momma." Rose could breathe again. Mission accomplished. But long after Momma left for the Quilting Society, Rose worried about what she might be doing and saying there.

Later that night, after her usual God bless Poppa, Momma, Aunt Norma, Uncle Ned, and all your defenseless creatures—especially horses, Rose added: And please, God . . . save us all from bloomer girl parades in Cape Light!

⚜ six ⚜

The next day, just before sunrise, Rose met Aunt Norma at the stables. The sky over the barns was becoming light with streaks of gold and pink. They walked down the long aisle between stalls and when they came to Midnight Star's, Rose reached over the door and offered Star an apple. The horse wouldn't come closer to her and though she was prepared for that—it was only their first morning together—she was disappointed.

"Put it in his feed bucket," Aunt Norma said.

Rose nodded. It always amazed Rose that Aunt Norma had such a strong resemblance to Momma, but a fraction of an inch here and a small difference there and her features added up to no more than pleasant. Rose wondered if it had been terrible for her to have a younger sister who was a great beauty.

"We feed a little and often because in nature horses

graze most of the day," Aunt Norma was saying. "Their stomachs need a steady supply of fiber for proper digestion."

"When he's in the pasture, he eats grass, doesn't he?"

"Grass by itself isn't nourishing enough. We feed the horses before they're turned out in the morning—breakfast is early around here, Rose—and again in the afternoon and evening. A mix of hay, alfalfa, and oats."

Rose listened carefully, but she couldn't keep her eyes off the sleek, muscular horse. Star stood motionless, ears back, the whites of his eyes showing.

"Give him bran mash once a week. I'll have one of the boys write down the recipe for you."

Rose nodded again. She needed to know all of this, but she couldn't wait to be alone with Star, to whisper sweet words and break through his stony reserve.

"Wait at least one hour after feeding before you exercise him. And never feed a hot horse. Make sure you cool him down after a workout. You don't want to risk colic. Am I going too fast, Rose? I know you have to get to school."

"I have time, Aunt Norma. I'm keeping track."

"Do you want me to have a stablehand take care of

his morning feedings? I don't want this to be too hard on you."

"Thank you, but maybe I have a better chance to reach him if it's me all the time." And I have to reach him very soon, Rose thought. Today is March twentieth; April twenty-eighth isn't that far away. "Anyway, my friends said they'd help."

"Even with the best of intentions, the chores might become a burden for them," Aunt Norma said. "All right, let's go on. Keep the feed buckets clean. And make sure he always has plenty of fresh water. You'll need to scrub out the buckets every day. I guess that can wait until the afternoon when you have time after school. And Rose, if you have any questions, find me or Uncle Ned. We're always around somewhere."

"I will, thank you."

"You know about mucking out a stall and laying down fresh straw, don't you? You can do that when he's outside in the afternoon. Groom him in the afternoon, too. Do you remember how?"

"I remember from last time I was here. With Summer Glory," Rose said.

"He's nothing like Summer Glory, Rose. Oh, he'll stand still for you, but only because he's frozen. He survived this far by controlling his emotions. He was smart enough to know he had no choice. If he misbehaved or tried to run, he'd be beaten."

Midnight Star seemed so alone. Motionless, quiet, afraid. Rose wanted to cry for him.

"You chose a horse with big problems, honey. You can change your mind."

Rose shook her head. "No. No, I won't let him go to slaughter!"

Aunt Norma looked at her sideways. "You know Ned is a good man, don't you, Rose? He told me about your agreement."

"You mean about waiting to sell Star at the horse fair?"

"I love Clayton Stables, but horses do have to be sold off. That's the nature of the business. Mostly it's to good homes, but sometimes it's heartbreaking," Aunt Norma said.

"I always thought I'd want to do what you do when I grow up. Run a stable or something like that," Rose said. "But not anymore. I don't think horses should be a *business*."

"Don't be so hard on us," Aunt Norma said. "Ned is honestly hoping with all his heart that you can make

Star seem more desirable at the auction in North Menasha. It's Star's best chance."

"Aunt Norma, do *you* think it's hopeless?"

"Probably." Aunt Norma glanced at Rose's downcast face. "But it's possible that Star might be more comfortable with a girl. I'd think his abuse was at the hands of men; the world of horses and of racing is all run by men. Except for me, of course." Aunt Norma grinned. "Though I stay quietly behind the scenes." She shrugged. "I don't know, Rose. Sometimes love can find a way."

I'll love him enough, Rose thought. "I guess I should get started."

"All right, then. I'll see you after school."

"Thank you." She watched Aunt Norma leave the stable, patting one horse's head and then another as she passed them in their stalls.

Rose took a deep breath. Now she was on her own. She opened the latch and entered the stall. She was dismayed by the way Star immediately shifted away from her. His only sign of emotion was the nervous flaring of his nostrils.

"My beautiful Star," she whispered. "You'll see. You'll be fine, we'll be a team, you and me, Star."

She raised her hand to stroke his shoulder—and

suddenly Star reared up! Rose's heart thumped wildly. He was towering over her. She was alone in a tight space with a nine-hundred-pound animal!

She gasped as she scrambled out of the stall and latched the door. Star's front hoofs came thundering down upon the stall floor, the place where she had just been standing. Her hand went to her throat. It was a while before she could breathe normally again.

Rose peeked over the stall door. Star's eyes, surrounded by their whites, showed his terror. She must have raised her arm too quickly. If a raised arm meant nothing but a beating to him—what had this horse been through?

"I only wanted to pet you," she whispered. How would she ever let him know that? He was too afraid. And now she was afraid, too. Could she make herself go back into that stall? But she had to, if she was going to feed and care for him. She had to!

She waited for Star to settle down. "It's all right," she said softly, over and over again. Finally, he seemed calmer. Now she knew never to raise her arm suddenly again. But if Uncle Ned had seen what had just happened, he would say Star was too dangerous and he'd make her stay away from him. Was there danger under Star's tense, too-quiet exterior? She didn't know. She only knew that this horse broke her heart and she wouldn't give up on him.

She *couldn't* be afraid! What had Uncle Ned told her when he taught her to ride? Horses pick up the subtlest gestures. You have to appear calm and confident. You have to be in charge.

Dear God, Rose prayed, please help me to be brave. Please help me do this one thing.

Rose straightened her shoulders and reentered the stall. Star turned his rump toward her and put his head into a far corner as though he hoped to disappear. He couldn't have made it more obvious that he didn't want her there.

She checked the feed bucket. It was empty and clean. Someone must have scrubbed it out earlier. She picked it up, careful to move slowly and quietly, and closed the stall door behind her.

She filled the bucket from the big metal bin at the far end of the aisle. She nodded to a stablehand who was crisscrossing from one stall to another. Horses' heads reached eagerly over their doors. Hooves stamped and pawed. "Easy, boy, breakfast coming up." She heard welcoming whinnies, the scrape of buckets and the soft sounds of munching. She took the deepest breath she could hold and filled her nostrils with the thrilling stable smells of sweet hay, ammonia, rich leather, and—horses! The morning sounds and scents of Clayton Stables coming to life. There was no place on earth she'd rather be.

Rose came back into Star's stall and again there was that that disheartening shift away from her.

The contented noises of other horses were all around her. Star gazed at the bucket. He moved his head sideways, keeping a wary eye on her. Rose thought, he's waiting for me to leave before he'll even eat! No wonder the stablehands and grooms didn't enjoy dealing with him.

She'd prepared herself not to expect twinkling eyes and sweet, warm nuzzling from him, not right away. But her entire body sagged with disappointment. She fought against feeling hopeless. It *had* to get better, though she had no idea of how to make it so. She remembered what Uncle Ned had said to her once: Horses don't forget but they forgive.

Again, Rose squared her shoulders. "You don't know it yet, Star, but you're my horse," she whispered. "I'll help you forgive."

Rose rushed to school from the stables and just missed the first bell. She dusted bits of straw from her dress and hurried into the classroom. Kat and Lizabeth waved, and Amanda smiled at her. Miss Cotter and Miss Harding ran a strict classroom—*no* talking out of turn. Miss Harding was in a bad mood and, left and right, knuckles were rapped with her ruler. Rose was kept busy with catch-up arithmetic exercises.

At recess most of the girls jumped rope. Mabel and Amanda turned the rope on either end and everyone chanted the words of a rhyme while girls jumped in one by one. Rose, waiting her turn, was alert for signs of a change in Kat, Amanda, and Lizabeth's attitude toward her, but everything seemed the same. Maybe they hadn't noticed how abruptly she'd rushed into her house yesterday. It was probably better not to bring it up or make excuses. She didn't have a good one, anyway.

Rose moved back in line to stand next to Lizabeth, and asked her, "Did your mother go to the Ladies' Quilting Society last night?"

"Yes, they meet every other Monday."

"Did anyone else go?"

Lizabeth looked at her strangely. "Well, of course. She's not the whole Society all by herself!"

"I meant . . . for instance, Kat's mother?"

"No, Aunt Jean's too busy with the lighthouse and

all." Whew, one less person to worry about!

"Did your mother say anything?" Rose asked.

"About what?"

"About meeting my mother."

"Oh, that's right, they met in the afternoon and again at the Society."

"What did she say?" Rose asked.

"That your mother's very stylish." Lizabeth's tone was definitely approving!

"Anything else?" Rose asked carefully.

"And . . . what else . . . oh, that your house is going to look lovely when— Oops, my turn!" And Lizabeth, with petticoats flying, jumped into the turning ropes.

It sounded like Momma hadn't said anything to offend anyone.

Rose felt a burst of optimism. Maybe Momma had finally realized, after all, that Cape Light was not the right place to push for the vote.

seven

When Rose and Kat arrived at the stables that afternoon, Star was out in the paddock. He was as sleek and magnificent a sight as the first time she saw him, but now Rose recognized his pained stillness in a field of carefree horses, and it squeezed her heart.

"Should we go to him and say hello?" Kat asked. "And pet him and—he's so beautiful!"

"I know, I want to. But I'd better get his stall done first," Rose said.

Rose used a pitchfork to muck out the stall and put the soiled straw into a lined wheelbarrow. Kat swept spiderwebs from the ceiling. Together, they covered the floor with a new, thick layer of clean straw and wood shavings for bedding.

It was awfully hard work, Rose thought, but there was something very satisfying about getting everything set up all clean and comfortable for Star.

Then there were the buckets to scrub out and refill. The two girls carried water from the well behind the stable.

"I'm sorry, Kat," Rose said. "It's heavy."

"That's all right." Kat smiled. "I like being here."

Rose smiled back. "I bet you'll love riding Star, and I'll teach you everything I know. When he settles down and relaxes."

But when they led him from the paddock to the stall, Rose wondered if Star would *ever* relax. He followed her lead obediently enough, but his body was rigid and Rose could sense his resistance.

The girls looked through the leather bag of grooming supplies and found a rubber currycomb, a stiff brush, a soft brush, a hoof pick, a mane-and-tail comb, sponges, and towels.

Rose started by standing at Star's left side, at his shoulder facing his tail. Picking out the hooves was the most important thing to do, but would Star let her? What if he reared up again? She mustn't let him know how anxious she was. Her heart pounded. If he lashed out at her, the sharp edge of a hoof could do real damage. . . .

With the hoof pick in her hand, she gently ran her

hands down his left foreleg and pinched the back of the leg lightly. Good, he'd been trained for this. He picked up his foot and she dug out all the packed-in dirt.

"*Whew*, he's letting me do it," Rose said.

"That's a good sign, isn't it?" Kat asked.

"Just his training. I guess he was given no choice." Rose checked the sole of the foot, the shoe, and its nails. She placed the foot back on the floor and, more confidently, did the same with his other feet.

"There's something so sad about him," Kat said. "Sad and lonely."

Rose went over his body with the currycomb, moving it in circles. "Maybe he'll get used to me." She remembered how Summer Glory had enjoyed being groomed. She could feel Star's tension whenever she was near him.

With a damp rag, Kat picked up the hair and dirt from Star's coat that had been loosened by the comb. "Don't you worry that his problems are too big?"

Rose nodded. "But I have to try to undo what was done to him." She bit her lip. "If I can save this one beautiful horse, maybe I'll stop feeling so bad for all the others."

"What others? What do you mean?" Kat asked.

Rose started with the body brush behind Star's ears and took long sweeping strokes in the direction of his hair. "I was on my way to a piano lesson and I passed a hill going up Broadway. It was just before Christmas and it had snowed the day before. At first, I just thought of how pretty everything looked, with icicles hanging from the fire escapes. And then I saw that the street was blocked with a traffic jam of carriages. The paving was covered with a hard coat of ice under a layer of snow."

Rose put the brush down and turned to face Kat. "The horses were floundering, straining up the hill, twisting and turning, doing their best to unclog the wheels. They were foaming at the mouth. And the drivers were furious and impatient. They were cursing and whipping the horses something terrible!"

"That's the worst thing, isn't it? When drivers are cruel," Kat said.

"Kat, I saw one horse slip. The cart overturned and his legs were splayed out to either side. He was helpless; he couldn't get up. And his driver was lashing and lashing him." Rose's eyes widened with remembered horror. "The snow around him was turning red! I cried out, 'Stop!' but no one paid any attention to me. Finally, I just turned away and went to my piano lesson. But I can't forget it. I should have done something to stop it."

"There was really nothing you could have done," Kat said.

"I don't know. Maybe not. But I wish I'd at least tried to do something."

"It hurts to be so soft-hearted," Kat said. "You feel everything double. But that's what I like most about you."

"Horses give and give. They're so willing and they try so hard," Rose continued. She ran her hand along Star's hide. She felt the hard, protruding ridges of the scars under his hair. "Kat, they're sensitive enough to feel the exact inch of skin that a fly has landed on." There was no doubt that Star had been viciously beaten. "I think the best thing that could happen for horses," Rose said, "is if automobiles spread everywhere and take over all the pulling and the carrying."

"That won't ever happen," Kat said. "Papa says automobiles are far too expensive and they always break down. Unreliable and noisy, too. They're just rich men's toys."

"But if I can save Star from slaughter, I'm afraid he'll become a carriage horse. He needs someone to appreciate and care for him."

"Now your story about the carriage horses is going to haunt me, too," Kat said.

"I'm sorry."

"Don't be sorry." Kat put her hand on Rose's shoulder. "It makes me want to do more for Star."

"Maybe helping just one horse doesn't make a big difference. But it does to me." Tears glistened on Rose's eyelashes. "It's the very best I can do."

"You'll get through to him, Rose, if anyone can," Kat said. "Amanda and Lizabeth will help, too. Between the four of us, we'll turn him around somehow!"

In the last two weeks of March, the grand old trees around the village square were pale green with new tender growth. Pussy willows lined the road that Rose took to the stables every morning before school.

Kat came most afternoons. She often brought her sketchbook and charcoals with her. Sometimes Kat sat on the top rail of the paddock fence and made quick drawings of the horses in motion. She was so talented! It made Rose wish she had as clear a direction for her life. Sometimes Kat sketched Star. She captured both his elegant conformation and his stiff, tense posture. Kat understands perfectly, Rose thought, and she liked her more than ever.

Amanda's little sister, Hannah, was enrolled in Uncle Ned's riding class for Thursday afternoons. That left Amanda free to join Rose and Kat at Star's stall. Amanda pitched in with the work whenever she could. She spoke to Star so kindly; how could he fail to respond to her, Rose wondered.

Lizabeth came, too. She didn't pretend to help muck out the stall or carry water buckets. Mostly, she posed prettily against the white fence of the paddock, wearing a smart new scarlet jacket and black velvet riding cap, along with shiny black boots and a long black skirt. She was the picture of what a fashionable horsewoman should wear.

"Are you going to take lessons?" Rose asked.

"No, I don't plan to actually *ride*," Lizabeth said. But she petted Star and talked to him, too.

Kat took time off to ride American Eagle and she came back to Star's stall with her face glowing. "It was so much fun! Your uncle was so nice to let me do that. As soon as I pay Todd back, I'm going to save for lessons. I want to be *good* at this!"

Rose grinned. "Now you've got horse fever, too!"

"Hmmm, I suppose riding could become popular for women," Lizabeth said. "Sidesaddle looks feminine, doesn't it? It doesn't seem that hard, and you don't have to get all sweaty and dirty, do you?"

"Hannah likes it a lot," Amanda said. "Maybe I'll try."

"The more you learn about riding," Rose said, "the more you realize how much more there is to learn."

"If you want to see some fancy riding, well, that horse fair in North Menasha isn't only about buying and selling," Lizabeth said. "I went last year. There are lots of riding events. Dressage and jumps and all kinds of demonstrations. You'll love it, Rose."

"No I won't," Rose said. "Not if Star is auctioned there."

"We can't let that happen!" Kat said.

"Not to Star!" Amanda looked distressed.

"We'll just have to think of something," Lizabeth said.

Rose was especially close to Kat but she felt lucky to have three such good friends. They all care about Star, Rose thought, and they're all encouraging me. But Star still glanced anxiously left and right, lifting his head up as high as possible to try to keep out of reach.

Rose couldn't wait anymore to ride Star. He had to be at least a little used to her by now. When she saddled him, she could feel his muscles tense up, but he stayed still. So far, so good. She walked him out of the stall and dragged over the mounting block. It was a nuisance, but she couldn't mount on her own unless she wore her riding skirt and she wasn't about to do that in Cape Light.

She put her feet in the stirrups and adjusted her position in the saddle. Riding sidesaddle made it harder to balance, but the worst part was that it made her too dependent on the reins. She couldn't use her legs to direct the horse, but she was careful to hold the reins with a gentle hand. Though Star instantly followed her directions, his body was rigid and his ears were pulled back. It was clear that he was unhappy to have her on his back.

They trotted around the paddock and Rose became as uncomfortable as Star seemed to be. She had done everything right. She had checked the girth strap to make sure that it wasn't too tight. She had placed the saddle blanket carefully under the saddle and smoothed away all the wrinkles. She was using the reins so gently—she knew she wasn't hurting his tender mouth. His stiff posture had to be simply because he wanted her gone. She took another turn around the paddock. There was no pleasure in it.

Finally, Rose dismounted and let him loose in the

pasture. Instantly he galloped far away from her. Rose's eyes suddenly filled as she watched him go.

"Oh Star, will you ever like me?" It was already March thirtieth. They had four weeks left.

~eight~

R ose came home from the stable one evening and called, "Anyone home?"

"In the parlor," Momma trilled.

The front hall was free of crates now. Their house was nice and orderly. She found Momma sitting at the ladies' desk in the parlor's bay window. Momma looked up with a brilliant smile.

"I had the most wonderful idea today, Rosie!"

"You did?"

"First, I should tell you. I finally found those pamphlets after all this time! It was the funniest thing . . . they were buried under some towels. I don't remember packing them with towels, but I guess I did everything in such a rush. I still can't find our tablecloths."

"Momma, I wish you'd get rid of them! The pamphlets, I mean, not the tablecloths."

"You know, I'm glad I had a chance to look them

over before I passed them out. They're a little . . . well, something more subtle might be better for Cape Light."

"Nothing at all would be best!"

"Now here's my idea. Rosie, sit down."

Rose sat down in a rose velvet chair alongside the desk.

"Look!" Momma handed her a card of creamy parchment. The writing on it was in Momma's elegant curly penmanship.

*Mrs. Merrill Forbes cordially invites you to a tea
in honor of her daughter, Rose . . .*

Rose looked up, confused.

Momma smiled. "Keep reading."

*. . . and to discuss the formation of the
Cape Light Girls' Club. Please join us
at our first meeting on . . .*

"Momma, what is this?" Rose asked.

"I'm starting a girls' club. For girls your age. I'll serve little cucumber sandwiches and pinwheel sandwiches, and strawberries and cream. How does that sound so far?"

"What kind of club?" Rose said slowly. Somehow she didn't think it would be about learning embroidery.

"Well, I thought, perhaps a weekly club? And we would talk about the importance of the vote and maybe have the girls write to congressmen. Between delicious refreshments and lots of fun, of course. It's so important to get the support of young girls just growing into womanhood."

"Oh, no!"

"Have you met Mrs. Cornell, the owner of the bookshop on Pelican Street? She thinks it's a wonderful idea, too. She helped me with the invitation list."

"No!" Rose shouted.

"But Rosie, it'll be fun and festive. You know I'm a good hostess. And I'll have little vases of grape hyacinths and violets at each place setting and—"

"No!" Rose screamed. She swallowed and lowered her voice. "What invitation list?"

Momma handed a sheet of paper to Rose. The name of every girl in her class anywhere near her age was on it!

"How could you do this without asking me? How *could* you?"

"I meant to ask you after school, but then you were

at the stables and I was so excited I couldn't wait to get started! I'd love to give a party for you, Rose. It's a nice way for you to make new friends and—"

"I don't want this. I really don't want this! *I'm* not the suffragist here! You can't get me involved. You can't get my friends involved!"

Momma's face fell. "Do you feel that strongly against it?"

"Yes!"

"All right, then. If that's the way you feel. I suppose it really is up to you." Momma sighed with disappointment. "Anyway, planning it was fun. But I used up my best stationery."

"Momma, none of those invitations went out, did they?"

"Just a very few. I haven't stamped and mailed them yet."

"A few? To whom?"

"Just a few girls, because I was passing their houses, anyway. I dropped them off. The mail takes so long and by the time—"

"Whose houses?" Rose interrupted.

"Well, Amanda Morgan, of course, because she's right across the street, and Lizabeth Merchant when I went to the bakery at the village green, and Joanna Mason. That's all, I think."

"You have to cancel, Momma. Make some excuse and cancel."

"All right. If you really want me to."

"I really want you to! Did the invitation say what *kind* of club?"

"No, just a girls' club."

Rose could breathe again.

"All right, I'll cancel it. I'll think of something. . . ."

Rose was too angry at Momma to stay with her for another minute. She was afraid she'd become seriously disrespectful.

"Is Poppa home?"

"In his office."

She rushed down the long hallway that separated their home from the waiting room and office. "Poppa, I've hardly seen you!" She smelled rubbing alcohol.

Poppa was arranging bottles of pills on a shelf of a white metal cabinet. "It's been busy. I met the doctor in Cranberry today, Dr. Clark. A pleasant elderly gentleman, but he's still using leeches for bad blood." Poppa sighed. "I thought I could wait a while to settle in, but the people here have been needing a doctor for too long."

He seemed tired but content. "I know they'll love you," Rose said. How fine he looked with his neatly trimmed mustache and beard and his brown eyes radiating kindness. On him, the Forbes nose was just right.

"I need to talk to you, Poppa."

"What is it, dear?" He sat down on the examining table and patted a spot by his side. "Tell me, how are you getting along?"

"Fine, Poppa, but there's one big problem." She sat down next to him. "It's Momma. It's starting all over again. She wanted to start a suffragist girls' club and I stopped her just in time! But who knows what's next? I know she'll talk to everyone about the vote, even to the new cook when she hires her, and—"

"I do hope that cook comes soon," Poppa said. "Putting a meal together is not one of your mother's best talents."

"Poppa, listen, she . . ." Rose lowered her voice. "She might even put on bloomers again! The other day she said, 'When it's appropriate'! Bloomers will *never* be appropriate! I'm afraid to bring any friends home. I don't know what she'll say or what she might be wearing!"

"Rose dear, you worry too much. Of course you can invite your new friends. They won't be concerned with your mother."

He didn't know, he had no idea! "What if someone finds out that Momma wears bloomers?" Rose whispered frantically. "Or about the arrest?"

"It was in the paper months ago, Rose, and I doubt that anyone in Cape Light gets New York City newspapers. If any of those papers are still around, they're lining the bottoms of birdcages."

"You're not taking this seriously enough! Poppa, please, can't you do something to stop her?"

Poppa smiled and patted her shoulder. "*Nothing* can stop your mother—neither man, nor beast, nor storm—if she believes it's the right thing to do. That magnificent spirit was why I fell in love with her in the first place. Well, that and her flashing gypsy eyes."

Rose sighed. Poppa would be no help at all! She should have known. He thought anything and everything Momma did was wonderful!

❧nine❧

Rose listened to Reverend Morgan in church on Sunday morning. "Hope," he said, "moves mankind forward and keeps us from sinking into despair. Hold on to your hopes with all your heart, but call on all your mind and strength to make them more than idle wishes." The minister looked around the congregation and smiled. "You hope that your boat comes home safely, but you'd better spare no effort to make sure it's shipshape before you set out."

Rose glanced at her parents sitting beside her. Momma nodded in agreement with the reverend. She certainly supported her hope for the vote with effort, though it was embarrassingly out of place. And Poppa hoped for better ways to treat terrible diseases like scarlet fever and smallpox. Rose knew he studied his medical books late into the night, looking for answers. My hope, Rose thought, is for Star to make a good impression at North Menasha and get a good home, but I don't know what to do to make that happen. Her *real* hope was to keep Star at Clayton Stables, and that seemed near impossible. She had to forget about her own feelings and focus on what was best for Star. She had to put her whole heart and mind into making him attractive to a nice buyer. Star needed more from her than idle wishes.

Rose glanced at Amanda. She was in her blue choir robe at the front of the church. Then she spotted that boy, Jed Langford, in the third row. He couldn't take his eyes off Amanda. And Amanda seemed flustered and trying hard not to look his way.

After services, Reverend Morgan stood at the church door to greet everyone as they filed out.

The Williams family came out and passed by the Forbes on the old stone steps. Mr. Williams was tall, with auburn hair just like Kat's. He was followed by Mrs. Williams, Kat, and her two younger brothers, Todd and James. Rose was wondering how she could greet Kat's mother politely and still avoid having to make introductions, when Mrs. Williams smiled at Momma and said, "Hello, Miranda. How nice to see you again."

Kat's mother had met Momma already! And now

Rose was forced to introduce Momma to Kat. After a while, Mr. and Mrs. Williams continued on their way, but Kat remained. She studied Momma, somehow looking more than just curious.

The memory of what had happened at Miss Dalyrumple's was still searing. Momma especially liked to preach about the vote to young girls. Rose had to do something, fast, before she got started!

"Sorry, we have to hurry right home," she told Kat. "Come on, Momma. Poppa, we have to go!"

Kat raised her eyebrows. "I don't mean to keep you. I just wanted tell you, Rose, we'll all be at the lighthouse later. It was a pleasure to meet you, Mrs. Forbes, Dr. Forbes."

The expression on Kat's face as she turned away made Rose's heart sink. Did her desperation to keep her wonderful new friends away from Momma make her behave so rudely that she would lose them anyhow? But what else could she do?

On the way home, Poppa asked, "What's going on, Rose? What was the rush?"

"Oh, because Star has to be fed and watered, even if it is Sunday."

"Are you really in that much of a hurry?" Momma

asked. "You were very abrupt. Don't you like the Williams girl?"

"I like Kat a lot. It's not that. I mean, it was because I want to take care of Star and meet my friends at the lighthouse later."

"She seems lovely," Momma said. "Maybe you could invite her for dinner sometime. Or lunch or—"

"No, she can't come, not ever, because . . . well, she has the early shift at the lighthouse."

"Oh. I see."

"Momma, how do you know Mrs. Williams? She called you Miranda."

"Mrs. Merchant invited me to tea last week and Mrs. Williams was there, too. They're sisters."

"Momma, you didn't bring pamphlets or anything like that with you, did you?"

"Why are you quizzing your mother?" Poppa asked.

"As a matter of fact, the only thing I brought with me was a nice box of cookies from the bakery. It was wrapped in the prettiest gift paper; I found out later it was hand-painted by your friend Kat."

"Did you . . . did you bring up anything about suffragists?"

"Only that it would be nice for *all* of us to have a say

in whatever Teddy Roosevelt does next. I was very subtle."

Rose groaned.

"It's just as well that we're hurrying home," Poppa said. "I'll have a quick lunch and pack a suitcase."

"Your shirts are ironed and ready," Momma said. "I hate to see you go."

"A suitcase?" Rose asked. "Where are you going, Poppa?"

"There are four cases of scarlet fever in Cranberry, Rose, and five more possible. I'm afraid it's spreading from down the coast. Dr. Clark needs help with the diagnoses and I'm going there this afternoon. I'll be in contagious sickrooms, so I'll stay away for a few days."

"I'll miss you so much," Rose said.

She'd been thinking about what to tell Kat. Maybe Poppa could be her excuse.

*

When the girls were gathered in the lighthouse tower that afternoon, Rose said, "Kat, about this morning after church. We were in a hurry because my father's leaving for a few days."

Kat shrugged. "You don't have to explain."

"But I want to," Rose said. "I know I must have seemed rude, but Poppa had to pack and—"

"Rose, your father looked as surprised by your big hurry as I was," Kat said. "I'm not *mad* at you. But either tell us the truth, please, or let's forget about explanations altogether."

Rose was taken aback. She'd felt so close to Kat. If Kat turned on her, she wouldn't be able to stand it. Was she imagining that Amanda and Lizabeth exchanged looks? Had they all been talking about her?

"Kat? Is there something else? I mean, what's wrong?" Rose asked.

"Well, it seems a little odd to all of us that you didn't invite Kat to your party," Lizabeth said.

"To my party?" For a moment, Rose was stunned. "Oh, my mother's tea! But that was canceled, wasn't it?"

"Yes," Amanda said, "but Lizabeth and I were invited —and not Kat?"

"Oh, that's because my mother hadn't mailed the invitations yet! But she dropped a few off to houses she passed that day—yours, Amanda's, and Lizabeth's, and Joanna's, that's all."

"Why *did* your mother cancel? The tea and the girls' club and everything?" Kat asked.

Rose was dumbfounded. She had no idea what excuse Momma had made.

"That's all right, Rose." Kat looked almost sympathetic. "I'm not blaming you for your mother. My guess is it was canceled because you got into an argument about inviting me."

"I don't understand. What do you mean?" Rose turned to Lizabeth and Amanda. "What did my mother tell you?"

"Just that she had a conflict with the dates," Amanda said.

"It doesn't matter," Kat said.

"But—" Rose started.

"I said it doesn't matter," Kat said. "Could we talk about something else?"

"But I don't understand what—"

"Rose, you're not ready to admit what's going on with your mother and that's fine. And I really don't want to talk about it anymore!" Kat turned to Lizabeth. "So, do you have another good book to lend us?"

There was an awkward silence. Amanda finally broke it. "Lizabeth has an account at the Pelican Book Shop," she told Rose, "and she passes her books on to us."

What does Kat know about Momma, Rose wondered. She felt panicky.

"I'm reading the best book," Lizabeth said, "but it's really thick so I'll take a while to finish. *Les Misérables* by Victor Hugo. That's French for 'the wretched ones.' "

"Not too hard to figure out," Kat smiled. "The miserables."

"I didn't like *Jane Eyre* that much," Amanda said. "Rochester wasn't nice at all, and I couldn't see why she loved him."

"I promise you'll like this one," Lizabeth said. "Anyway, Jean Valjean steals a loaf of bread and he's arrested, but he escapes and the policeman hunts him for years and years. He just won't let go! Once you get into it, it's very exciting. Do you think someone should be jailed for just a loaf of bread?"

"Stealing is stealing," Amanda said.

"Even if someone's hungry?" Kat asked. "That's unfair."

"You still have to obey the law," Amanda said. "If someone's arrested, there's a good reason for it. He's a criminal."

Rose squirmed. She wished they would talk about something else.

"In the book, you're on Valjean's side," Lizabeth said, "though in real life, you wouldn't want anything to do with a jailbird. You can't have jailbirds running around loose."

Rose's throat felt tight. What if they found out about Momma?

"Don't worry, Lizabeth, we don't have any convicts in Cape Light." Kat laughed. "Anyway, someone innocent could be arrested."

"Valjean wasn't innocent," Lizabeth said.

"But if he's never forgiven," Kat said, "and the policeman goes on hounding him forever . . . What do you think, Rose?"

Rose felt as though a too-bright light was being focused on her. She blinked. "Think about what?"

"About convicts and jailbirds."

"I don't think about that!" Rose exploded. "Why should I? Jailbirds. What a dumb thing to talk about! Who cares what anyone thinks about convicts and jailbirds!"

Rose suddenly realized she was shouting. She clapped her hand over her mouth.

In the silence, Kat, Amanda, and Lizabeth looked at each other.

Rose couldn't face their startled looks. She jumped up. "I have to go."

ten

Kat didn't come to the stables every afternoon anymore. Rose missed her.

"Do you want to walk over with me?" Rose asked her after school one day.

"No, I can't."

"You can't?"

"I'm busy with my gift wrap," Kat said.

Rose suspected that Kat continued to help with Star's care occasionally only because she had promised she would.

I'm not about to force myself on anyone, Rose thought. She no longer spoke to the girls with the same easy confidence. She could no longer say, "Let's go see Star" or "Are you going up to the tower? I'll meet you later." Rose held herself back. She waited for the girls to approach her. Sometimes they did and sometimes they didn't. More and more, she was alone with Star.

Rose thought she felt him relaxing, but by such a small fraction that she wasn't sure if it was wishful thinking. She combed out his thick black forelock and gazed into his eyes.

"Monday, April ninth," she whispered. "We only have three weeks left." She loved the warm breath from his nostrils. "Please, Star, trust me not to harm you."

She'd have to try again to show Star that someone in the saddle didn't have to mean harsh treatment. Instead of tugging the reins, it would be so much better to direct him with properly placed, gentle pressure from her legs. Of course, that couldn't be done sidesaddle. Rose sighed. She'd have to get the divided skirt from the back of her closet. She couldn't possibly let anyone see her in it! But if she changed at the stable and back again before she left, no one would know, except Kat, Amanda, and Lizabeth if they came by.

After school the next afternoon, Rose was heading home to pick up the divided skirt when she saw Amanda and Hannah ahead of her on William McKinley Road. They were going toward Lighthouse Lane. Should she hurry to catch up and walk with them? She was so uncertain. Even after Rose's outburst in the tower, Amanda had continued to be friendly, but maybe that was just her gentle, well-mannered way. Maybe she thought Rose was too peculiar. . . .

Hannah was lagging behind; Amanda stopped and turned back.

"Rose!" Amanda waved. "Aren't you going to the stables?"

"Not until later. I have to stop at home first."

"Oh, good, then we can walk together! How's Star?"

"About the same," Rose said.

"I'll bring an apple for him when I come Thursday," Amanda said.

"Me, too," Hannah piped up. "I love horses! I love Nellie the best!"

Amanda smiled. "You've made Kat horse-crazy, too."

"She hasn't come by very much," Rose said cautiously.

"That's because of her gift wrap. Didn't she tell you? Last week, she finally finished a last-minute order for Easter."

"Oh. I didn't know."

"So cute, with little rabbits in all different colors. I guess you didn't see them. You haven't been up to the tower in a while."

"Well, I've been busy with Star. And then homework and—"

"Can I run ahead?" Hannah asked.

"May I," Amanda corrected.

"*May* I," Hannah echoed. "Well . . . can I run or not?"

Amanda laughed. "All right."

They watched Hannah streak away.

"Rose, what's wrong?" Amanda asked.

"Nothing." Rose shrugged. Then, finally, "Kat's . . . um . . . different. Is she angry with me?"

"No. She decided she doesn't blame you."

"Blame me for what?" Rose asked.

"Well, I might as well go ahead and say it." Amanda sighed. "We've all noticed that you don't want to invite us over. And then, when Kat wasn't invited to that tea and it was canceled so fast . . . Well, she thought it was because of your mother."

For a horrible moment, Rose couldn't breathe. "My mother?"

"You and Kat were becoming so close and . . . well, Kat thought maybe your mother didn't like that because your father's a doctor and hers is just the lighthouse keeper."

"No! That's not true!" Rose said. "She's wrong!"

"But Kat decided it's not your fault. You're not responsible for how your mother feels. But you know, Kat loves her father more than anything and her pride was really hurt."

"She's so wrong!" Rose said. "My mother's not like that!"

Amanda looked at her curiously. "We don't really know what your mother's like."

"She's not a snob! Not at all! Please, tell Kat—"

"I think you'll have to tell her yourself," Amanda said.

Rose sighed. How could she explain? What could she say?

They had reached Amanda's cottage. Hannah bounced inside, and the door slammed behind her.

"Oh, look," Rose said. There was a bouquet on Amanda's doorstep, a bunch of pussy willows held together by a bedraggled ribbon. Hannah had just missed stepping on it.

Amanda picked it up and bit her lip.

"Is there a note?" Rose asked.

Amanda shook her head. "I know who it's from. At the barn dance last fall, I told Jed I love pussy willows even if they're not flowers. . . ." She turned the bouquet around and around in her hand. "He remembered." Her eyes were suddenly shiny with tears.

"Amanda, what is it? Aren't you glad that he—"

"I don't know what to do! That night, we danced together all evening, from the Virginia reel all the way to 'Good Night, Ladies,' and we talked and—it was so wonderful! The very best evening of my life!"

"Well, then why aren't you happy?"

"Father didn't notice. But later Mrs. White mentioned it to him and he said it was improper for me to dance with the same boy all evening. That I shouldn't have done that. And he's told me I'm too young to even think of courting, not until I'm sixteen, at least close to marriageable age. I want to please Father more than anything in the world and I don't ever want to disappoint him. But I'm only thirteen, Rose! Does that mean I can't see Jed at all?"

"I don't know." Rose was touched by the misery in Amanda's eyes. "Maybe . . . maybe you could see Jed sometimes. Would your father have to know?"

"I can't do that! I won't go against his wishes. And Rose, the worst part . . . " Amanda was suddenly blushing. "I held hands with Jed," she whispered. "Just for a little while, when we were walking. And then I read in the *Ladies Home Journal* that hand-holding was improper unless you're officially engaged! I'm the minister's daughter and I need to set a good example and I'm failing miserably!"

"You're not, Amanda! You take care of Hannah so cheerfully, without any complaints ever, and you keep house and—"

"I keep thinking about Jed." Amanda's eyes were downcast. "I don't mean to, but I do. I miss my mother so, now more than ever."

"Amanda, I'm sorry."

"Lizabeth looks down on Jed because he's just a deckhand and Kat never cares about what's proper, but I have to talk to someone! I thought you, coming from New York City and all, you'd know about boys and flirting."

"I don't know anything about boys." Momma would be the perfect person to advise Amanda, Rose thought, but of course that would be impossible!

"I have to prepare Hannah's snack." Amanda fingered the bouquet nervously and a soft gray bud fell to the ground. "I don't know what to do with this." She sighed. "Well, see you tomorrow."

"See you tomorrow."

Rose crossed Lighthouse Lane. She opened the

front door of her house and started up the stairs to her bedroom. Momma's voice was coming from the parlor and the words Rose heard made her stop short.

"And then there were two absolutely burly policemen, holding me by each arm . . . " Momma's lighthearted laughter was punctuated by the sound of tinkling teacups. "And they actually *handcuffed* me! Can you imagine? Miranda Forbes, dangerous criminal on the loose!"

Rose's face became red-hot. What was Momma *doing*? Who was she talking to? Rose crept down a few steps to take a peek. Mrs. Cornell, the owner of the Pelican Book Shop, and another lady she didn't recognize were sitting on the sofa. This was Rose's worst nightmare come true!

"And they actually dragged me from the parade and *arrested* me and charged me with assault, disorderly conduct, and resisting arrest!" Momma's carefree laugh pealed again. "Oh, and indecent exposure because of my bloomers! It wasn't funny while it was happening, I was too furious, but now, after the fact . . ."

Rose sank down on the stairs and buried her head in her arms. She couldn't face it! Momma was revealing everything!

Did she think she was entertaining them? Now everyone in Cape Light would talk about their worst secret. What would Lizabeth, Amanda, and Kat think? And Mrs. Williams? And Reverend Morgan? Mrs. Merchant? Her teachers? It was all too horrible to imagine! The Forbes family might as well pack up and leave right now! How *could* Momma do this to her? Again!

Rose had exactly the same horrible, stomach-turning sensation that had engulfed her when she'd read the article on page seven of the *New York Daily Mirror* last November.

". . . the spitfire wife of well-known physician Dr. Merrill Forbes . . . suffragette parade along Lexington Avenue . . . With sharp raps of her umbrella, Mrs. Forbes injured two gentlemen bystanders along the parade route . . . overnight in a holding cell at the precinct until Dr. Forbes arrived to collect his combative lady . . ."

Rose heard footsteps, good-byes, and finally the front door opening and closing. She ran down the stairs in a fury.

"Rosie? I didn't hear you come home," Mother called.

"Of course you didn't! You were too busy spilling all the family secrets!"

"Oh, you mean—" Momma came to the foot of the stairs. "Mrs. Cornell and Mrs. Lancaster were here. Have you met them yet? Why didn't you come into the parlor?"

"Because I was too ashamed to face them!" She just couldn't hold her tongue any longer. "How could you? How could you *tell*? Now it will be all over Cape Light!"

"Mrs. Cornell and Mrs. Lancaster are my best friends here, and are completely sympathetic to the suffragist movement. In fact, Mrs. Cornell is going to join me in—"

"I'll be completely humiliated! And Poppa, too! Everyone will know!"

"I absolutely trust Mrs. Cornell and Mrs. Lancaster not to gossip." Momma extended her arm toward Rose. "Don't you give me any credit for common sense, Rosie?"

"No!" Rose was red-faced. "I've done everything I could—*everything*—to keep people from . . . from knowing about you and now you. . . . Oh, what's the use!"

"If you're embarrassed by me, that's too bad!" Now Momma's eyes were blazing, too. "I'm not planning to shout it from the rooftops, but I'm not the least ashamed of anything I've done. If you care to remember, I was defending myself against—"

"I don't care to hear it again!" Rose's voice was cutting. She'd heard the story before, and too many times at that.

She could recite Momma's excuses in her sleep: Yes, thousands of men had lined the parade route to jeer at the suffragists. Yes, many of these men had been drinking quite a lot. Yes, some of them thought these liberated and bloomered women were inviting physical contact. Yes, the police officers had little experience with such unladylike behavior and they didn't protect the women properly. And yes, when two of the men along the route poked and prodded Momma, she whacked them soundly with her umbrella.

"Whether you want to hear it or not, I have nothing to apologize for," Momma said. "It was lucky I had the umbrella with me. That cut scalp—I believe it needed several stitches—and that black eye were richly deserved!"

"If you hadn't been parading in the first place," Rose said, "none of it would have happened. 'Spitfire wife!' 'Combative lady'! I don't see how Poppa could hold his head up after the newspapers ran the story!" It enraged Rose that Poppa, instead of putting a strict stop to Momma's activities after that awful incident, said he was proud of her courage!

"I can't believe a daughter of mine cares more about what people think than about what's right! The right to vote *matters* and you have to be willing to take risks for—"

"It doesn't matter to me! I don't care. You're ruining my life!" Rose shouted. "I wish I had a normal mother like everyone else!"

Momma's eyes widened and Rose bit her lip. She knew she had gone too far.

They stared at each other in silence over the stairs that separated them. Rose gripped the banister.

Then Momma said, her voice even and very low, "You are a huge disappointment to me, Rose. A huge disappointment."

There we are, Rose thought. I'm not the daughter she wanted and I never will be. I don't care about politics or voting and I care too much about what people think to ever run around in bloomers! Finally it's out. The plain, awkward daughter with the Forbes nose is a huge disappointment.

Rose knew that she had to get away before she exploded. To Star and the stable! She grabbed the divided skirt from her room and ran from the house.

eleven

ose leaned against the side of the stall as Star finished munching oats from his bucket. At least he wasn't waiting for her to leave before he ate. That was something, she supposed, though not very much.

Everything possible was going wrong. Star was still a frozen horse she couldn't reach. Her fresh start in Cape Light had turned sour—from an explanation she didn't know how to give to Kat, to the story about Momma that might be all over town in a day. The thought of Momma's words made her wince. Rose wished Poppa were home. She believed Poppa loved her, but she wasn't even sure of that anymore. If she was such a huge disappointment to her own *mother*, why would anyone else care for her?

"Oh Star . . . Star." Rose put her arms around the horse's neck. She was so all alone, she needed comfort from any warm body, even from a horse that shrank from her. Well, no, he wasn't moving away so much right at this moment. "Star, what am I going to do?"

She combed his mane and his forelock. She concentrated on what she was doing and tried to empty her mind but the lump in her throat grew and grew and finally erupted in explosive, heaving sobs. She buried her face against Star's neck and bawled. She shook with sobs, her nose ran, her eyes leaked uncontrollably, and rivers ran down her cheeks.

It was a long time before she could make herself stop. Her breath came in long gasps. And it was combined with other breaths, the warm, moist breaths from large nostrils against her neck. Star's head was weighing down her shoulder. Star was nuzzling her!

Rose kept very still, afraid to spoil the fragile moment. She looked into Star's lovely long-lashed eyes. The far-away expression was gone. His eyes held hers.

Had the weeks of patience and kindness finally reached him, by coincidence, at this particular time? No. Rose knew this as clearly as she'd ever known anything: Star felt her distress, just as she had been feeling his. The expression in his eyes showed kinship.

Her tears had left a dark, damp mark on Star's coat and she smoothed it with her hand.

Star nickered—what a sweet sound!—and pressed

against her. In spite of everything, he was taking a chance and offering her his affection and trust. Fierce joy swept through her.

Rose wiped her eyes with the back of her hand. "Thank you, Star."

He needed to be exercised, she needed to change his water, but for now, she stretched her arms along his side. His hair was bristly against her skin and smelled of the pasture: grass, hay, and sunshine. Her long, dark hair, fanned out upon his coat, blended with his black mane. They relaxed together in the afternoon quiet of the stable, broken only by Star's released sigh and the buzz of a fly.

Rose knew that if she rode him now, whether sidesaddle or whatever, he would respond—but she wanted to do this right, with her best skills.

"I'll be right back, Star," Rose said, smiling. "Don't go away."

Rose shut the door of Star's stall and went down the stable aisle into the storage area that served as a tack room. It smelled deliciously of leather and saddle soap. In a dark corner, she changed quickly out of her petticoats and normal skirt, and put on the divided skirt. It was made of soft tan leather. She actually loved the way it felt against her skin, though of course it was a most peculiar thing to wear. She liked walking with the new freedom it gave her, but she'd never want anyone in Cape Light to see it. She put on her riding cap with the hard crown in case of a fall. She peered around the door. No one was nearby. The stablehands must be feeding horses housed in the other stables. Riding school was in session at the far end of the property. She was safe from disapproving eyes.

Star welcomed her back with a soft whinny; how heartwarming that was, especially because she had given up on ever being greeted by him!

She put the saddle pad in place on Star's back and checked to make sure it wasn't bunched up when she put the saddle over it. She strapped the girth around his belly and slid her flat hand between the girth and the horse. Good, not too loose and not too tight. She led him out of the stall and mounted. She didn't need a mounting block, everything was so much easier when she could use both her legs!

Now her thighs and knees rested against Star on either side. Rose held the reins lightly and squeezed with her lower legs. Star responded immediately by walking. Rose closed her left hand on the reins, eased with her right hand, pivoted her head and shoulders to the left and squeezed and released with her left leg. Star made a smooth left turn onto the path. "Good boy!" This was so much better for his tender mouth than directing him by yanking on the reins!

Rose squeezed with her legs and pushed with her back; Star began to trot on cue, not like the perfectly trained, miserable machine he'd shown her before, but as her willing partner. Rose found Star's rhythm. She followed his motion, moving her hips forward and pivoting from her knee. She felt his eagerness to run, but she kept him in a slow trot to warm up.

They left the paddock area and cantered along the trail leading away from Clayton Stables. "All right, Star, here we go!" They crossed a meadow and Rose asked for a gallop. Star stretched out with flowing speed, running smoothly with easy freedom. This was not like the frenzied racing Star had been forced into, Rose thought, this was willing, joyful running. Rose laughed out loud with pleasure, her wind-whipped black hair mixing with Star's flowing black mane.

There was no past and no future, only this harmony with speeding hoofbeats. She knew Star could feel her breathing, as she could feel his. Riding him was a dance with the perfect partner. In the saddle, Rose thought, is the only place I've ever felt graceful.

They passed through fields in a blur of green and brown. They had gone almost as far as Cranberry before Rose turned back.

They were cantering through another meadow when she saw the hedge in the distance. Would Star jump? Everything seemed possible on this miraculous afternoon. She'd take the risk. She couldn't resist trying.

They continued toward the hedge at a steady canter. Rose was in half-seat, arching her back and letting her heels drop down with each stride. She felt the proper lock between her upper calves and the horse. She aimed Star straight for the center of the hedge. Three strides before the hedge, they picked up speed—too late to change her mind—and then the crescendo into the jump.

Star raised the front of his body and pushed off with his hind legs as she rose out of the saddle and moved forward to follow the horse. They sailed over the hedge in one fluid movement. This was as close to flying as riding could get! Star landed on the other side with perfect follow-through in three fast strides.

"Beautiful, Star!" His form was flawless; he must

have been taken over hundreds of jumps before. "You wonderful, wonderful horse!"

When they came close to Clayton Stables, Rose slowed him to a cool-down trot. How sweetly he followed her slightest command! Then a walk on a loose rein around the paddock.

"Rose!" Kat was sitting on the top rail of the fence. "I couldn't find you and Star anywhere."

"We had the most thrilling ride!" Rose dismounted and led Star to his stall. "The *perfect* ride. He's a brand-new horse. Aren't you, Star?" Rose glowed with pride in him.

Kat followed. "When did that happen? I missed everything, didn't I?"

"Just now, this afternoon," Rose said.

"Do you think kindness just finally reached him?"

"Something like that," Rose said. She couldn't describe what had passed between her and Star.

"That's the best news!" Kat said. "And you're wearing your riding skirt. I like it!"

Rose smiled at Kat, then ran her hands along Star's body. Slightly damp with sweat . . .

"I scrubbed out the water bucket and filled it," Kat said.

"Thank you."

"I didn't mean to break my promise to you," Kat said, "about helping. I had an order to finish and—"

"I'm not holding you to a promise." Rose rubbed him with a dry towel. "Come only if you want to, Kat."

"Well . . . do you want me to?"

"Yes, I do." Rose took a breath and plunged in. "Amanda told me what you've been thinking. Kat, you're wrong. I can't talk about the reason now, but if . . . if I act strange sometimes, it has nothing to do with you or our fathers. Nothing."

Kat looked at Rose, listening carefully.

"Whatever else is wrong with my mother, she's not a snob. She's not like that at all, I swear to you."

"Then what is it?"

"I can't tell you." Rose swallowed. "I can't." Kat would know her secret, along with everyone else in town, if Mrs. Cornell and Mrs. Lancaster started talking. But maybe, just maybe, they wouldn't. She had to hope they wouldn't. "But it's not about you. Honestly."

Rose used the hoof pick, starting with Star's left foreleg. She kept her eyes on the clump of grass and mud wedged into his shoe. "I felt . . . well, especially close to you, I guess." She couldn't quite face Kat. She was asking Kat to put up with a lot, no questions asked. "I want nothing more than to stay good friends." Then the right foreleg. "I don't know how you feel about that."

"It's all right," Kat said.

Rose could finally look up at her.

"I *was* wondering, though, when you were so upset about jailbirds . . ." Kat leaned closer, excitement in her eyes. "Rose, are you hiding an escaped prisoner? And bringing him food in a hideout?"

"No, of course not. I'm sorry, Kat, I can't talk about it."

"I said, it's all right."

"Is it?" Rose asked.

Kat nodded. "Maybe someday you'll trust me."

Kat reached out to pet Star's muzzle. He shifted away from her and raised his head out of reach.

"I guess he's a one-girl horse," Kat said.

Rose couldn't help being pleased. There was something special just between Star and her and no one else! But then she bit her lip as a new realization took away all the happiness of the afternoon.

"Kat, nothing has changed after all," Rose said slowly. "I don't think Star could handle the riding school. Strangers. New riders yanking at him or making mistakes would set him right back to where he was. Uncle Ned will see that in a minute. Kat, there's still no place for him at Clayton Stables."

"Oh, Rose."

"I've done him no good at all."

"Yes you have! Didn't your Uncle Ned say he'd have a better chance if you socialized him? Well, he's socialized, isn't he? Sort of."

"Sort of," Rose said. She thought of how he'd nuzzled her and their sweet communion.

"And now he has a much better chance to get a nice buyer at the horse fair. That's helping him, Rose."

"That's betraying him. We don't know who's nice. Kat, I can't do that to him. I can't let Uncle Ned sell him!"

⊱twelve⊰

The front parlor was freshly painted a pale yellow. The dark velvet drapes had come down, replaced by white linen. Their home looked light and cheerful now, but that was misleading. Rose and Momma were hardly speaking to each other. Poppa was still gone, and the house felt chilly and too big for the two of them. Of course, there was Edna, the new cook, and Momma had hired a cleaning girl. Goodness only knows what Momma's telling them, Rose thought. Rose escaped to the stables every chance she had. She wished she could have her meals there, too. Eating with Star would be a lot more comfortable than sitting silently across the table from Momma and seeing the disappointment in her eyes.

Whenever Rose arrived at the paddock, Star would trot directly to her at the fence, happy to see her, whinnying his greeting. No matter how bad everything else was, riding Star was a joy for both of them. A joy, Rose knew, that was coming to a painful end. April eleventh, April thirteenth, April sixteenth . . . The horse fair in North Menasha was less than two weeks away. And then an idea came to her. Not perfect, but it might protect Star . . .

Rose found the parts for an X-jump under some horse blankets in a corner of the tack room. Amanda and Kat helped her carry the upright end poles and the horizontal poles to the pasture. Even Lizabeth helped to set them up when Rose showed her how.

"See, the poles rest on the cups," Rose explained. "That way, if the horse hits the poles, they'll just fall down."

"It still doesn't look safe to me," Lizabeth said.

Rose had to see how Star would handle the X-jump. They cantered toward it. She adjusted his stride, put him in the correct spot to take off—and Star traced a perfect, smooth arch over the top! Star made her look better than she was, Rose thought. Whatever she lacked in experience, Star made up in willingness and intuition. Or maybe he'd even been used in steeplechase races. She'd never know. He was magnificent! She had to make sure that everyone would see that.

She slowed down in a big circle and they came to a stop in front of the girls.

Kat was impressed. "You have to show your uncle. That has to change his mind about Star."

Rose dismounted. "One jump won't make a difference to him. I don't want him or Aunt Norma to know what I'm doing. Not yet. I'm afraid they'd make me stop. They might say it's dangerous—and I can't stop, I have to *practice!*"

"Practice?" Amanda asked.

Rose stroked Star's soft muzzle. "If I can't keep him, I want whoever buys him to *know* how wonderful he is. So that if he's difficult or skittish, they'll be patient with him. And treat him well." Her voice began to crack. "They have to see Star at his best, so they'll remember what he can do. And I'm going to show them."

"How?" Kat asked.

"Uncle Ned said the horsemanship events come before the auction," Rose said. "I'm going to be in the jumping event with Star so I can show him off to everyone at North Menasha."

Amanda, Lizabeth, and Kat didn't respond. Rose was disappointed. It *was* a good idea, she thought. Anyway, it was the only one she had.

"I'll have to wear this"— Rose indicated her divided skirt —"in *public* and it's going to be so embarrassing, but there's no other way. And maybe there's a tiny chance if we win—suppose the blue ribbon—maybe Uncle Ned will agree that Star is much too special to sell." That bit of hope allowed Rose to smile a little. "Well, what do you think?"

Lizabeth shook her head.

The divided skirt was bothering Lizabeth, Rose thought, and it was bothering her, too, but embarrassment was nothing compared to her love for Star. Awful as it would be, she'd wear it in public for him. But why was Kat shaking her head, too? Kat didn't care anything about what was proper.

"Kat?" Rose asked.

"It's a good idea," Kat said slowly, "but there's a big problem."

"A problem?"

"All the events, dressage and jumping, all of them, are for boys and men only. That's the way it's always been."

"But . . . but that's not *right*!" Rose sputtered. "I can jump as well as a boy. And if I can't, I should at least have the right to *try*! Well, shouldn't I?"

"I know; it's not fair," Kat agreed, "but they'll never let a girl register."

Rose led Star back to his stall and the other girls followed.

"But it's the only way I can help Star! And Star is a good jumper. This is his chance to shine! What difference does it make if a boy or a girl is in the saddle?"

"Maybe they have to protect women from danger," Amanda said.

"I can decide if I want to take a risk, can't I? I don't *want* to be protected!" Rose knew she was going on and on, but she was too upset to stop. "I'm sorry, but I'm *furious*. A completely stupid rule is stealing Star's best chance and I can't let that happen! What does being a girl have to do with riding—or anything?"

An unwelcome thought crept into her mind: What does it have to do with *voting*? Maybe this fury I'm feeling is what makes Momma behave the way she does, Rose thought. Of course, the horse show is an entirely different situation. Momma isn't saving anyone. She's selfishly doing whatever she wants without caring how it affects me!

That evening, in the midst of the dinnertime silence between Rose and Momma, the front door creaked open.

"Poppa!" Rose got up from the table and flew into his arms.

He put one arm around Rose's shoulders and the other around Momma as he walked them back into the dining room. "How are my girls? I missed you."

"And I missed you," Rose said. "I'm so glad you're back!" She wanted to tell him how awful Momma had been.

He sat down at his place at the head of the table. Rose waited until Edna served the crabmeat appetizer and went back to the kitchen. She was about to speak up when she noticed how his shoulders were sagging. It seemed that new lines had been etched in his face. He looked pale and exhausted.

"It was bad," he was saying. His voice was hoarse. "All I could do was sit at their bedsides and try to give comfort."

"I'm sure you helped, Merrill," Momma murmured.

"No, medical science is painfully ineffective against scarlet fever." His deep sigh was full of discouragement. "Some people recover, others don't, and all my training makes no difference. There was one beautiful little boy, a three-year-old with black hair and bright, mischievous eyes—until they became hollow and faded with the fever. I had no way to save him, Miranda. I keep hearing his mother's agonized cries. . . ."

"You did your best, Poppa." It shocked Rose to see how haunted his eyes were.

"My best wasn't good enough," he said. He bent his head to say grace. Momma and Rose followed his lead.

"Thank you, God, for the bounty we are about to receive," Poppa said. "Thank you for this family, so fortunate to be together tonight and free of illness. Dear God, I pray for more knowledge and advancement in science. Please bless and comfort those who are bereaved tonight. Amen."

Rose couldn't complain about Momma, she decided, not when Poppa was just back from so much tragedy. Rose looked at Momma and their eyes met. Momma extended her hand toward Rose. Almost without meaning to, Rose stretched her arm. Their fingertips touched across the table.

Rose was grateful they were all healthy and together, but that didn't make everything all right. She could forgive Momma for being a suffragist and at least there were no jailbird rumors circulating around town. Mrs. Cornell and Mrs. Lancaster hadn't gossiped. But Momma's terrible words still smarted. Whenever Rose thought of "huge disappointment," she wanted to either cry or break something.

thirteen

ose saw signs for the horse fair posted all around the village green. There was one in the barbershop's window behind the red-and-white pole. She saw another one over the pickle barrel inside the general store/post office when she picked up her family's mail. She read the sign once again in the bakery shop window. Kat's words: "They'll never let a girl register," echoed in her mind and made even the delicious scent of hot-cross buns seem sickening.

NORTH MENASHA HORSE FAIR
Come one, come all!
Saturday, April 28, 1906—Angel's Field, North Menasha
Dressage, Jumping, Cross-Country Races
Noon–3:00 PM
Sale and Auction 3:30 PM
Registration for riders
Monday April 23–Friday, April 27
10:00 AM–6:00 PM, North Menasha Town Hall

There was more information, about refreshments and pony rides, but Rose's eyes were fixed on the registration dates. It was already Wednesday, April twenty-fifth! Registration was going on *right now*—and without her!

~

"I'm watching the week of registration slip away," Rose told Kat, Amanda, and Lizabeth. They had gathered in the lighthouse tower after the stables on Thursday afternoon. "And I'm helpless."

Amanda nodded. "And tomorrow's the last day!"

"I can't *stand* thinking of other horses on the course, horses not as good as Star, only because their riders are boys! I need this chance to show him off!"

"I don't remember seeing that many great riders last year," Kat said. "And the two of you together . . ."

"I do believe that seeing Star perform would make someone appreciate him and be kinder to him. If someone doesn't know any better, he can seem like a difficult horse. What if he's whipped again? Or traded for slaughter?" Rose turned away to hide her tears. She went to the window and looked at the ocean pounding against the rocks below.

Rose couldn't stop imagining Star's bewilderment

and fear, his ears pulled back and his eyes wide and rimmed with white. There had to be something she could do. There had to be *something*!

"Listen, everybody, I have an idea!" Kat said. "It may sound a little crazy—all right, a lot crazy—but I don't see why it can't work. At least, listen before you say no."

"What? What is it, Kat?" Lizabeth asked.

"What if Rose dresses like a boy?"

Rose whirled around. "You mean wear *trousers*?"

Kat looked at the startled faces. "Well, if you can pass as a boy just long enough to register and be in the jumping event—"

"I could never do that!" That would be like wearing *bloomers*! The thought was too horrifying. "That *is* crazy!"

"It's a terrible idea," Lizabeth said. "Completely unacceptable. If Rose were discovered, she'd be disgraced."

"She'd never live it down," Amanda added. "No decent girl—"

"But if she's *not* discovered," Kat interrupted, "there she is, taking Star over the jumps! It's risky but . . ."

"I can't," Rose said. "I can't risk making a spectacle of myself in front of everyone. I'm new here and—I can't!"

"You're right, I guess it was a terrible idea." Kat shrugged. "Forget it. It would take an awful lot of courage to go that far against the rules."

Rose turned back to the ocean, churning inside as much as the waves below. She loved Star but . . . No, she couldn't do it. Kat might be brave enough. And Momma—well, Momma plunges into things without thinking twice. I'm not like them, Rose thought. I worry about what people think of me and I want to blend in.

"Anyway," Lizabeth said, "what would she wear?"

"Between my brother and yours, we could put something together," Kat said.

Lizabeth raised her eyebrows. "Todd is ten years old and Christopher is twice her size. It won't be easy finding something to fit."

"Stop! We're going to forget about it, aren't we?" Amanda said. "Why are you still talking about it?"

"You're right," Kat said. "There's no point. "

The only place I'm brave is on horseback, Rose thought. But how could she let Star, bewildered, be auctioned off, his reins held by an uncaring stranger, while all sorts of people shouted their bids? If there was even a slim chance to make it better for Star—maybe even a slim chance to convince Uncle Ned to keep him! There was something about being here in the lighthouse that made her reach deep inside herself for courage.

Suddenly Rose turned and blurted out, "I'll do it!"

"You will?" Lizabeth said. Amanda looked shocked. Kat applauded.

"Then we'd better get busy," Kat said.

"Tomorrow's the last day, just until six," Rose said. "I don't even know the way to North Menasha."

"I'll go with you," Kat said. "There's a four-thirty train out of Cranberry. It's a short ride, we'll make it there in plenty of time."

Then everyone was talking at once.

"I'll go, too," Lizabeth said. "I do admire your nerve! We'll bike to the Cranberry station. Amanda and I can take the two of you on our handlebars. No, *I'll* ride on the handlebars."

"We'll meet here *immediately* after school," Kat said. "I'll bring Todd's clothes, and Lizabeth, you bring Christopher's."

"He'll kill me if he ever finds out," Lizabeth said. "He gets mean if anyone touches his things with even a pinky finger!"

"I don't approve at all," Amanda said, "but I'm not letting you face this alone, Rose. I'll arrange for Hannah to play at Mary Margaret's tomorrow."

"I'll ask Aunt Norma to take care of Star in the afternoon," Rose said.

"And I'll get Todd to stand by for my shift at the lighthouse," Kat said.

"What about Rose's hair?" Amanda asked.

"Cut it!" Lizabeth said.

"No!" Rose screamed. "Not my mane!"

"We'll tuck her hair into Todd's newsboy cap," Kat said.

"I'll bring my hairpins," Lizabeth said. "This is exciting!"

Hairpins were forever falling out of Lizabeth's pompadour. What if my hair falls down, Rose thought. She was going to go through with it but would anyone believe she was a boy?

❦ *fourteen* ❧

They left Amanda and Lizabeth's bicycles at the Cranberry station and scrambled onto the four-thirty train just in time.

"We made it!" Kat's eyes were sparkling. "We're on our way."

"I love traveling on trains," Lizabeth said.

"Look, there's the high school going by!" Amanda was glued to the window, watching the scenery speed past.

Lizabeth laughed. "The school isn't going by. *We* are."

The whistle blew twice as the train rounded a curve.

"This is such fun!" Kat said.

Even Amanda was caught up in the excitement. Only Rose sat very still and quiet. Along with being scared and worried, she was itchy and too hot—the fault of Todd's knickers. In the lighthouse tower, Rose had tried on a pile of clothing. Christopher's trousers were much too long and the pants legs looked ridiculous rolled up. Todd's clothes were tight, but she'd managed to get into these black-and-white wool tweed knickers. There was no other choice.

It was unseasonably warm for April and the knickers were thick and itchy. She'd be sweating even if she was calm—which she certainly wasn't. The wool newsboy cap that hid her hair made her that much hotter. She wore a long-sleeved blue striped shirt of Christopher's. Her arms were too girly, Kat said, and she had to hide them. The shirt was too big, but Lizabeth said it didn't look terrible tucked in. To go with it, Lizabeth had brought Christopher's blue tie. Leave it to Lizabeth to have everything match, even for a disguise! They almost missed the train because it took them so long to figure out how to tie a tie. Todd's kneesocks and shoes—too small, her feet were cramped—completed her outfit. Rose was hideously uncomfortable.

Rose sneaked a look at the other passengers in the car. One had his nose in a book and the other four were busy talking to each other. They weren't looking her way, but still . . .

"Kat, the outlines of my *limbs* show," Rose whispered.

"That's all right, boys' knickers show their legs," Kat said.

"But I'm not a boy," Rose whispered. "If anyone knew—" It would be a huge scandal. "It's—it's almost like being naked!"

"Well, that's what Lady Godiva did on horseback, isn't it?"

"Kat!"

"Rose, if no one knows you're a girl, it won't matter."

"What if . . . I think impersonating someone is against the law," Rose said. Could she be *arrested* for pretending to be a boy? She shuddered. A jailbird: like mother, like daughter!

"If you register as yourself, that's not impersonating," Kat said, "What's your middle name?"

"Lorraine. Rose Lorraine Forbes."

"All right, you're R. L. Forbes." Kat grinned. "What's wrong with that?"

"Wait! What about my voice?" There were too many things they hadn't thought of that would give her away in a minute!

"Hmmm. What can we do about Rose's voice?" Kat

asked Lizabeth and Amanda. "She might have to answer a question or . . ."

"Easy," Lizabeth said. "She has terrible laryngitis. We have to speak for her—I mean, him."

Rose nodded. "All right, that's good." She took a deep breath and fanned herself with her hand. I can do this, she told herself, and tried to relax back into her seat. "Maybe I can pass as a boy."

"I think so," Lizabeth said, "though you're an odd-looking boy."

"You're much prettier as a girl," Amanda added.

"Pretty? *Me*?" Rose was stunned.

"Don't pretend you don't know that," Lizabeth scoffed.

"Those high cheekbones are an artist's dream," Kat said.

"My nose," Rose mumbled. "I have an awful profile."

"No, you don't!" Kat laughed. "Seriously, I'd love to paint your portrait sometime."

"Don't let her," Amanda said. "She'll make you sit absolutely still and—"

Amanda was interrupted by the conductor. "Menasha!" he called as he strode through the cars. "Menasha!" The train pulled into the station.

"Oh, good, we're here!" Lizabeth said.

They gathered their belongings and scurried off the train. Except for Rose, who couldn't *scurry* in Todd's shoes. They forced her to take awkward, somewhat pigeon-toed steps.

They blinked in the sunshine on the station platform. Amanda checked her wristwatch. "A quarter to five. It *was* a short ride."

"Oh, no." The dismay in Kat's voice made everyone stare at her. "This is *Menasha.* We wanted *North* Menasha. The next stop."

They watched helplessly as the train chugged from the station and became smaller and smaller in the distance.

"Well . . ." Lizabeth swallowed. "We'll have to wait for the next train."

"The next train won't be for hours," Kat said.

"Registration closes at six," Rose said. "I *have* to register today!"

"North Menasha is walking distance," Kat said. "We can still make it."

Amanda shook her head. "I know the way, but we have to take Pequod Boulevard and that curves all around before it ever gets to North Menasha; it'll take forever!"

"No good. We have to go a direct way," Kat said. "Through the woods." She pointed to the trees that surrounded the station.

"Through a *forest*? Do you actually know the way?" Lizabeth asked.

"All we have to do is follow the train tracks. We know we have to go north, don't we? How hard can that be?" Kat answered.

They entered the patch of woods alongside the station. It was mostly scraggly trees, hardly a forest. There was a well-worn dirt path and they could easily see the train tracks through the thin brush. They walked in the direction the train had gone.

"My *shoes*!" Lizabeth complained. "I wasn't planning to *hike* today!"

My *feet*, Rose thought, I'm getting blisters.

"Oh, come on," Kat said. "We'll be there in no time."

But then the path veered off at an angle. The girls stopped.

"The path or the tracks?" Amanda asked. The brush had become dense.

"The path. There's nowhere to walk along the tracks—look, it's all thick brambles," Lizabeth said. "My dress will be ripped to shreds!"

"I guess you're right," Kat said. "The path has to lead somewhere. I bet it comes back around to the tracks."

"As long as we know the direction we're going in," Rose said.

"We're definitely heading north," Kat said.

They set off without speaking, moving ahead determinedly. The silence was broken by snapping twigs underfoot and the constant buzz of insects. The woods became denser. The deep shade was a relief to Rose; her face was flushed with overheating, and drops of sweat trickled down her arms.

And suddenly the path ended in the middle of nowhere.

"What now? Should we try to get back to the tracks?" Amanda asked. "They're to our left, aren't they?"

"I'm not sure," Kat said. "The path turned the other way, didn't it?"

"If we try to cut across to the tracks, we'd be going out of our way, wouldn't we? I think we should go ahead to get to North Menasha," Rose said.

"We could go back the way we came," Lizabeth suggested. "On the *path*."

"But then we'll never get to registration in time," Rose said. "What time *is* it?"

Amanda checked her watch. "Five-twenty."

"We have to hurry!" Rose said.

They rushed forward, pushing their way through bushes. Branches tugged at them. Rose tripped over a log, and when she straightened up she saw crawly things coming from the moss under it. They looked for clear spots to place their feet.

"Everybody, stop!" Amanda called.

"We can't, come on," Rose encouraged.

"No, stop. I mean it," Amanda said. "See that oak tree? We passed it ten minutes ago. We've gone around in a big circle."

"That's impossible," Kat said. "There are hundreds of oak trees, Amanda."

"But I know *that* one because, see, there's that longish nest hanging from the fifth branch up and I wondered what it was."

"There are hundreds of nests, Amanda," Kat said, but she sounded less confident.

"Not in a tree with white violets at the base," Amanda said. "And a big mushroom growing on the trunk. I *know* this is the same one."

"I think that's a wasp's nest." Lizabeth's voice quivered. "Let's keep walking."

"Fine," Kat said, "but in what direction?"

"You mean we're *lost*?" Lizabeth asked. "I *told* you we should stay on the path and go back the way we came!"

"Told-you-so's won't do us any good now," Kat said. "I suppose we could keep walking until we reach . . . um . . . *something*."

"We might reach *nothing* and just get deeper into the forest," Lizabeth said. "It'll get dark and if there are mountain lions—"

"There are no mountain lions in Massachusetts!" Kat said.

"Just because you haven't seen one . . ." Lizabeth said.

"Please, don't argue. We have to think," Rose said.

"Maybe we should stay put until someone finds us," Amanda said.

"Why would anyone in their right mind ever come here?" Lizabeth said. "We may have to eat berries and moss to stay alive and . . . and they might not find us until spring."

"It *is* spring," Kat said. "Lizabeth, could you please stop?"

"That's it! Moss!" Rose said.

Everyone looked at her. "What?"

"I remember exactly what to do," Rose said. "Everyone, look for trees with moss growing on the trunks."

"What? Why?" Kat asked.

Lizabeth's eyes became huge. "We're not really going to eat moss, are we?"

"No," Rose said. "Moss always grows on the *north* side of a trunk. That's a fact. So we'll know which way to go."

"That's brilliant," Kat said. "How did you know that?"

"And a New York City girl, too!" Amanda marveled.

"My old school had Nature Lore in Central Park," Rose said.

They found moss on tree trunks and—Rose breathed deep with relief—it was all growing on the same side. The fussy Nature Lore teacher knew what she was talking about after all!

They headed north with new energy. How far off did we wander, Rose worried. Will we actually get to North Menasha? And if we do, can we make it to Town Hall before six o'clock?

fifteen

"That big white building in the distance," Rose said. "Is that the town hall?"

They had finally reached Constitution Street in North Menasha.

"That's it, straight ahead," Kat said.

"Rose," Lizabeth said, "you're not walking like a boy."

"Well, what am I supposed to do?" Rose cringed with embarrassment when they passed other people on the street.

"I don't know, but you're walking like a girl," Lizabeth said.

"Tread heavily and swing your arms," Kat instructed. "Walk like everyone else is supposed to get out of your way."

"Forget about *walking*," Amanda said. "It's ten to six. We have to run!"

"I can't run and I can't *tread* either, whatever that is! Todd's shoes are killing me!" But Rose gritted her teeth and kept up with the others with a peculiar loping gait.

It was five minutes before six when, out of breath and gasping, they reached the columns in front of the town hall. Kat stopped everyone. "We have to get ourselves together. Rose, tuck in your shirt."

Lizabeth pushed Rose's stray hair back under the newsboy cap and looked at her critically. "This is the best we can do."

"I'm . . . I'm scared," Rose whispered. "I don't think I can . . . "

Kat pulled her inside the building. The main entrance of the town hall had an impressive marble floor. Todd's shoes squeaked. Rose winced with each step.

Kat took a step into the only open door off the entrance and the others followed.

"Yes, may I help you?" a lady behind a desk said.

"We want to—I mean, our friend wants to register for the horse fair. For jumping."

"Charlie! Another one!"

The man called Charlie was at a coatrack at the

side of the room. He was shrugging a seersucker jacket over his shirtsleeves.

"We're closing," he said.

"Sir, it's only five to six," Lizabeth insisted.

"Three to six now," Amanda whispered.

"Sorry, girls, there's a chicken pot pie waiting for me."

"But sir, our friend came all the way from Cape Light," Kat pleaded.

"Walking most of the way," Lizabeth muttered.

"Please, sir," Amanda said with her most appealing smile.

"All right, all right, hurry along. Let's make this fast." He led them to a desk at the side of the room and pulled a notebook out of a drawer. His eyes slid past Kat, Lizabeth, and Amanda. Then he spoke to Rose. "Which event?"

"Jumping," Amanda answered.

He flipped a page in his book. "Name?"

"R. L. Forbes," Kat said.

The man stared at Rose. "What's the matter with you, boy? Cat got your tongue?"

"He's got awful laryngitis, sir," Amanda said. "He can't speak at all."

"What's the *R* stand for?"

There was a pause.

"Come on, come on, what's his first name?"

"Um . . . Ro," Kat said.

"Row? As in row your boat?"

"That's why everyone calls him R. L.," Lizabeth explained.

"Horse's name, age, gender?"

"Midnight Star," Amanda said, and then she looked at Rose. Rose whispered in her ear and Amanda continued, "Five years old, gelding."

The man scribbled on a yellow card and handed it to Rose. "Here you are, be sure to have it with you. You're last, number ten. Angel's Field. Jumps are first, twelve noon. Good night."

Rose frantically tugged at Kat. "Ask him when I can see the course."

Kat and Rose ran to catch up to the man at the door. "My friend wants to know when sh-*he* can see the course."

"It'll be set up by ten tomorrow morning." He took a closer look at Rose. "There's a lot more wrong with you than laryngitis, boy. Looks to me like you've got a serious fever."

Rose wiped the sweat from her brow. Before anyone had a chance to even thank him for his time, the man was gone.

On Constitution Street, Kat, Lizabeth, and Amanda giggled and skipped. Rose limped along, giddy with relief.

"Good thing he was in a hurry," Amanda said.

Kat laughed. "We're lucky he loves his chicken pot pie."

"And I have an entry card!" Rose waved it in the air.

They laughed and congratulated themselves all the way back to Cranberry on the train.

"We pulled it off!" Kat said when they stepped onto the sidewalk at the Cranberry station.

Rose loosened the tie. "But what if I can't pass tomorrow?"

"Don't worry so much." Kat took Rose's hand and gave it an encouraging squeeze. "You did fine today. You were really brave."

Suddenly a deep voice called, "Lizabeth?"

Lizabeth gasped. "Oh, no, there's Christopher!"

Kat dropped Rose's hand as if it were a hot coal.

Two boys came toward them. One had black hair, brilliant blue eyes, and even features. He was the more handsome of the two, but there was something about the sandy-haired boy that made Rose's heart race. His brown eyes glinted with mischief and his crooked grin signaled a private joke. He looked rather wild and full of devil-may-care confidence. Incredibly, he seemed to be drawn to her, too. He was staring straight at her!

Lizabeth made quick introductions. "My friend R. L., my brother, Chris, Chris's friend Michael Potter, from Cranberry."

"We just came from *The Great Train Robbery* at the nickelodeon," Chris said. "It was good. It had a real story, not just scenes." He was talking to everyone, but he kept glancing over at Rose. And Rose could only think, Oh my, the exciting sandy-haired one is Christopher Merchant, Lizabeth's brother! He put her brain in a jumble.

"One time, the actor pointed his gun straight at the audience. It looked like it was coming through the screen." Chris laughed. "People screamed and one lady ran out. Lizabeth could have gone into her phony swoons."

"I don't do that!" Lizabeth protested. She swallowed. "Anymore."

"What are you doing in Cranberry, anyway?" Chris asked.

There was an uncomfortable silence as the girls looked at each other. "We were planning to go to the nickelodeon, too, " Kat finally said.

"You're too late, Katherine," Michael snarled. What had Kat ever done to him, Rose wondered.

Then Chris said. "R. L.?" He scratched his head. "Something's very familiar about you."

Oh! She was dressed as a boy in *his* shirt and tie! *That's* what he'd been staring at! Lizabeth was well aware of it and trying to rush him on his way. "So long, Chris. See you at home."

The other boy, Michael Potter, had been glaring at Rose all along. He looked at her so furiously that it was scary. What was that about? "So long," he muttered and stalked away.

But Chris said, "Wait a minute, Mike." He turned back to Rose. "You're from Cape Light?"

Rose nodded. She blushed under his scrutiny.

"I've never seen you before, have I?"

Rose shook her head.

"But something's awfully familiar—can't put my finger on it. . . ."

Rose shrugged. Not only was she wearing his shirt, she was sweating in it!

"You're a friend of my sister's? Why haven't I heard of you?"

Rose shrugged again.

"What's the matter with you? Don't you *talk*?" He turned to Lizabeth. "What's the matter with him?"

"He has awful laryngitis," Lizabeth said. "Michael's *waiting* for you, Chris! I'll see you later!"

They watched Christopher take his bicycle from the station rack. After a few words, Michael walked away around the corner.

"Want to ride home with me?" Christopher called.

"No!" Lizabeth said. "I'll see you later!"

"All right, but—" Christopher took another long look at Rose. "Something weird there . . ." he said as he rode away.

This is too awful, Rose thought. The most interesting boy I've ever met and look at me! Kat's face was red, too. She had never seen Kat so upset. What was going on?

Amanda noticed. "Kat, what's the matter?"

"Oh, nothing, just that Michael saw me holding hands with R. L. and I can't imagine what he thinks!"

"Oh," Rose said. "So that's why he looked as if he wanted to punch me! He must like you a lot."

"I don't know. Maybe he did *before* he saw me

with . . . If he did, that's all ruined now, isn't it? Well, I don't care," Kat said. For someone who didn't care, Rose thought, she was taking it hard.

Amanda and Lizabeth looked confused. "You only saw him that one time at the barn dance," Lizabeth said, "for about two seconds, and you never talked with him, did you?"

Kat cleared her throat. "When we picked apples at Potter's Orchard last year—Mr. Potter is his uncle—Michael was there. I guess we talked a little when I went to get a ladder."

"You never said a word to us!" Lizabeth said.

"Why did you keep it a secret from me?" Amanda asked. "I mean, if we're truly best friends . . ."

"Because it wasn't important. I don't care *anything* about Michael Potter! Not a bit!"

"If we'd known you like him, we could have fixed it," Lizabeth said. "We could have explained *why* you were holding hands with R. L."

Kat looked curious. "And why would that be?"

"Well, to *comfort* him for . . . for . . . " Lizabeth frowned. "For his laryngitis!" she finished triumphantly.

"What a great fix!" Kat laughed in spite of herself. "That'll teach me to keep secrets from my best friends."

Kat's secret was only a tiny one, Rose thought, but mine is huge. Trust is what friendship is all about. If she was afraid to invite Kat, Lizabeth, and Amanda to her home, what kind of friendship was that? She wanted Kat, Amanda, and Lizabeth to be her best friends forever and ever. Someday they were going to have to meet Momma. . . .

"Let's go," Amanda said. "I have to get dinner started."

"I can't wait to get home and get out of these things," Rose said.

"You'll have to come to the lighthouse and change into your normal clothes first," Kat said.

"No, I'm going straight home," Rose said.

"But if your mother sees you like that, you'll be in big trouble," Lizabeth said.

Rose hesitated before she said, "No, I won't."

"You won't? My mother would be horrified," Kat said.

"Father would never let me out again," Amanda said.

"My mother's not like that," Rose said.

"What *is* she like?" Amanda asked. "We don't really know her."

"Don't be silly, Rose," Lizabeth said. "Anyone's

mother would faint if her daughter came home in knickers!"

Rose took another deep breath. "Not mine."

She couldn't deny Momma forever. She couldn't keep lying and hiding and being so fearful. It didn't feel good. If she could muster the courage to be R. L. and enter herself for the horse fair, she could do this. Rose drew herself together.

"My mother is a bloomer girl."

~sixteen~

"My mother is a bloomer girl. A suffragette."

There was a stunned silence.

I need their help so badly at the horse fair, Rose thought, and if they turn from me now . . . What have I done?

Kat was the first to finally speak. "How wonderful! I can't wait to talk to her!"

"She can't be," Lizabeth said. "I've seen her in church and never in bloomers."

"She doesn't wear them all the time." Rose swallowed hard. "Mostly for demonstrations and such."

Amanda frowned. "Cape Light won't take kindly to bloomers or demonstrations."

"I know," Rose said miserably.

"It must be terrible for you," Amanda said. "Your own mother!"

"I can't believe it," Lizabeth said. "That blue suit she

wore in church last Sunday had to be straight from Paris, France! She's *beautiful*, and suffragettes look more like men than ladies, don't they?"

"No, they're all kinds of women," Rose said.

"Mrs. Cornell, from the Pelican Book Shop, for instance," Kat said. "She's very feminine and attractive, but she's for suffrage. She got into a debate with Ma about it."

"Was . . . was your mother very angry at her?" Rose asked.

"No, I think they agreed to disagree. . . . Oh, now I get it!" Kat exclaimed. "Is that why you never invited us to your house?"

Rose nodded.

"I can understand that," Lizabeth said. "I'd die of shame."

"I'd be *proud*," Kat said.

"Will you . . . will you still help me at the horse fair?" Rose asked.

"Of course! Poor Rose," Amanda said. "We'd never blame you for what your mother does. We like you, no matter what."

"I'm glad you trusted us enough to reveal the skeleton in your family closet," Lizabeth said. "We're still your friends."

Kat laughed. "It's not a *skeleton*. It's only about wanting to vote, for goodness sake! I'm glad you finally told us."

"I know that real friends have to trust each other," Rose said. She was so relieved; it was easier than she'd imagined.

Kat nodded. "I'm lots more comfortable without all the mystery."

"Come on," Lizabeth said, "let's get going." She and Amanda went to the bike rack.

"Why were you so afraid to tell us?" Kat asked. "What did you think would happen?"

"In my old school, I lost all my friends."

"Just because of your *mother*?" Kat asked. "No one's responsible for their parents' behavior! Lots of them are peculiar, one way or another."

"My mother came home from a parade one afternoon. In *bloomers* and some girls from my school saw her." And then Rose remembered the bad things she'd said about Abigail's mother. If she had just quietly defended Momma and not attacked Abigail's, then it might have been different. She'd never know for sure, but she couldn't keep blaming only Momma.

"That afternoon, when we were talking about *Les*

Misérables and you got so upset . . ." Lizabeth and Amanda were still out of earshot and Kat leaned close to Rose, her eyes gleaming. "I think I get that, too! I'm only guessing, but . . . Was your mother ever *arrested* in a suffragette demonstration?"

"Something like that," Rose admitted.

"I think we'll keep that to ourselves," Kat whispered. "But your mother is wonderful. What spirit and adventure! I wish my mother could be exactly like her. Ma's too old-fashioned. She wants everything to stay exactly the way it was in 1900!"

"And I've been wishing that Momma was exactly like *your* mother!"

❦

Rose came home footsore and bedraggled.

Momma was in the front hall. In one quick glance, she took in Rose's outfit. "What in the world— Rose, what is this?" She started to laugh. "Is this your version of the bloomer girl look?"

"No!" Rose said. "It's not *funny*!"

"Sorry, I shouldn't laugh, but you really have to explain this to me." Momma led her to the sofa in the parlor. "Why are you hiding your hair? What were you doing?"

Rose sank down and pulled off the newsboy cap as hairpins flew everywhere. It felt good to have hair tumbling over her shoulders again. She took off Todd's shoes and socks—something she'd normally never do downstairs, but she couldn't wait another second. "I had to dress as a boy to enter Star in an event."

"Oh, Rosie, look at your poor feet." Momma massaged the ball of her right foot and Rose gave in to the comfort in her touch. "Tell me about it. What event?"

In a torrent of words, everything that had happened poured out of Rose. "It makes me so mad! What does being a boy or a girl have to do with riding in the horse show?"

"Absolutely nothing. Nor with voting, nor any number of unjust laws," Momma said. "Here, give me your left foot. Look at those cramped little toes."

"I guess it really does matter whether women are equal citizens," Rose said. "I can see that it makes a difference in everyday life." That was a big concession from her.

Momma gave Rose a big, pleased smile. "That's what I've been fighting for." She gently flexed Rose's toes. "Any better now?"

Rose nodded. "I'm not a fighter. I want to pass just

for tomorrow, for Star's sake, and then I never want to see knickers again! How can you stand wearing bloomers?"

"They're loose and very comfortable. Those knickers are too tight for you, and wool tweed at this time of year—"

"They itch!"

"I don't see why you'd wear them again," Momma said.

"I *have* to, for tomorrow!" Didn't Momma understand anything that Rose had told her? How important it was for Star?

"Let me see that entry card," Momma said.

Rose handed over the yellow cardboard square.

"Look!" Momma's smile was triumphant. "It states the *horse's* gender—gelding—but nothing about yours. Nothing here says you're a boy. Not one word!"

"But it's understood," Rose said.

"But there's nothing actually written here to keep you from riding as *yourself*! As a girl. It's a grand opportunity to make a strong point for everyone to see!"

"I don't *want* to make a point." Rose pulled her feet back and tucked them under her. "That's the last thing I'd want to do! I don't *want* anyone to notice me. I'm doing this only for Star!"

"I suppose you're not ready," Momma said. "I'd hoped you—"

"You only think about the suffragist movement," Rose said. "You don't consider me at all!"

"Do you truly believe that?" Momma studied her face.

"You'd let me be disgraced just to make your point."

"Rose, why do you think I'm a suffragist? Why do you think I care so deeply?"

"I don't know. Because you like the attention or—"

"Because I have a *daughter*! Oh, Rosie, it's for *you*. I thought you knew that. Rosie, I'm all grown up and lucky to be married to a wonderful man who gives me as much freedom as he can. It's *your* life that I'm thinking of! I want you to have choices and rights—whether it's riding in a horse show or electing your representative or legally owning property. It's all for you!"

Rose was as thunderstruck as if a bolt of lightning had just shaken the parlor. She stared speechlessly at Momma.

"I'm sorry, Momma," she finally said. "I didn't understand." I never really understood how much courage it takes to go against popular opinion, Rose thought. North Menasha gave me just a tiny taste. No wonder Poppa and Kat admire Momma's spirit! "I'm sorry. I'm not that brave. I can't take a stand tomorrow."

"Trying to pass as a boy takes nerve enough," Momma said. "I'm very proud of you, Rosie."

For a moment, Rose was lulled into leaning against Momma but then she quickly sat up. "Proud?" She felt terribly sad. "But I'm still your huge disappointment."

"What do you mean?" Momma asked.

"'You are a huge disappointment to me.' Your words, Momma." The weeks of bottled-up hurt came spilling out. "I know I'm plain, with the Forbes nose, and too tall and thin. Don't you think that disappoints me, too? But for my own mother to say that!"

"Oh Rosie! How could you think—" Momma shook her head. "I was hugely disappointed that a daughter of mine didn't think it was important for me to stand up for what's right. I was hugely disappointed that embarrassment would make you crumble and say the vote didn't matter." Momma passed her hand over her forehead. "Maybe I was harsh, but it isn't easy to know that your own daughter wants to hide you away."

"Is that really all you meant?" Rose asked in a small voice.

"Of course. And you're not plain! Where did you ever get that idea?"

"I've always known. When I was very little, two of our relatives—I don't remember which ones—were looking down at me, tsk-tsking, 'Too bad the child has the Forbes nose and the mother's such a great beauty.'"

"As if a small child can't hear or feel anything!" Momma exploded. "You never had a cute, baby-doll look. Your beauty is very individual, interesting, and strong. You have to carry it with confidence. And you'll grow into your body. You're like a young colt who starts off all legs. Rosie, you're *lovely*!"

"Am I? Mrs. Merchant is always telling Lizabeth how pretty she is. You never say anything like that."

"I suppose I don't very often." Momma sighed. "Physical beauty is a gift to be grateful for, I won't deny that. But you know, I've spent most of my life trying to get people to see beyond that and take me seriously. Your father was one of the few men who didn't treat me as a piece of decoration. The things that matter most to me are brains and character. I'd never think to praise 'prettiness.' " Momma put her arms around Rose. "I'm so sorry I hurt you. I never meant to."

Rose snuggled into the hug. "I'm sorry, too, Momma."

Momma smiled. "And now *you're* standing up for what's right, in your own way." She smoothed back

Rose's hair. "I'll go to the horse show in the carriage with Poppa and Norma. Are you coming with us?"

"Oh, no, I have to be there early, to check the course. Please don't say anything to anyone."

"Don't you want to tell Uncle Ned and Aunt Norma?"

"No, I'll surprise them. No one should know ahead of time that I'm entering as a boy. Please don't tell, Momma."

Momma nodded. "All right, I won't. When the time comes, we'll be there cheering you on."

Momma knew very little about horses or jumping. But if Uncle Ned and Aunt Norma knew what she was planning, they were sure to stop her. Rose knew they'd think Midnight Star was still too skittish to be trusted over jumps. They'd say it was too dangerous.

Rose wasn't worried about *danger*! She had too many other worries. She had to get to North Menasha early and get Star and herself ready. Ugh, boy-clothes. She had to pass at the event. She had to do well!

❧seventeen❧

Rose was at the stables before dawn on Saturday. She mucked out Star's stall and layered the bedding of straw and wood shavings with a catch in her throat. By the end of the day, there might be another horse in this stall. She leaned against the wall and took in Star's contented munching, his occasional nickering in her direction, and the smell of horse and fresh hay. Maybe for the last time. She didn't think she could bear to come to the stables again if Star wasn't here.

She'd found Uncle Ned at one of the other barns earlier that morning. He had planned to ride Star to North Menasha in time to take a look at the horses for sale before the show events began. Rose had convinced him to let her ride along with him on Star. "Our last ride," she'd pleaded and he agreed. He'd ride Monogram. They would arrive at eleven, only leaving an hour for Rose to walk the course and change her clothes, but it would have to do. If she begged Uncle Ned to leave much earlier, he'd wonder why.

Rose gently worked out the tangles in Star's mane. Star looked at her with sweet, loving eyes. Rose held back the tears behind her own. She plaited his tail. She put grooming supplies and a small bottle of oil in a bag along with Todd's knickers and Christopher's tie; she'd do last-minute brushing at the horse fair to remove the dust of the road. "Someone has to see your beauty and your talent and your heart. Someone *has* to love you."

Now there was nothing left to do but wait for Uncle Ned. She put her arms around Star and rested her face against his warm hide. She half-closed her eyes. "Remember I loved you, Star," she whispered. "Remember I did my best." Deep in her heart of hearts, she wouldn't say good-bye. Just maybe, if they jumped the course brilliantly, maybe Uncle Ned would keep him. . . . Star is good enough, but I'm not an expert, she thought in despair. But I'm all he has.

Rose was as ready as she could be without alerting Uncle Ned. She wore Christopher's shirt tucked into her divided riding skirt. She was going to be comfortable on the long ride, no matter what anyone thought! Her riding boots replaced Todd's shoes—thank goodness, with room for her toes! The hard riding hat was on her head. At the last minute, she'd make the quick change into knickers and Lizabeth would pin up her hair. Kat, Amanda, and Lizabeth would be there to help her.

Rose and Star rode to North Menasha at the leisurely pace that Uncle Ned set. She was anxious; she still had so much to do!

Uncle Ned looked at her sideways as they trotted along. "I know you've gotten through to Star. Everyone at the stables says you have quite a way with horses. You did a good job, Rose."

"Good enough to—" Rose started hopefully.

"I'm sorry, no," Uncle Ned said. "He's still too difficult with everyone else. What can I do with a one-girl horse? I'm sorry, Rose. I'm not keeping him."

❧

When they arrived at Angel's Field in North Menasha, Uncle Ned led the way to the holding pen for the horses to be auctioned. All sorts of horses, all sizes and shapes, with saddles removed, moved about restlessly.

"We're early, they're not all here yet," Uncle Ned said. His expert eye scanned the available stock. "You want to ride Star in, Rose? Take off his saddle and everything else of ours. Just leave the bridle and reins so he can be led to the auction."

There was a closed gate with a watchman. If I take Star in, she thought, I won't be able to get him out! He'll be released only to a buyer or his legitimate owner!

Uncle Ned noticed her hesitation. "I shouldn't have let you come," he said. "I'll take care of it, you can run along." His voice was scratchy. "I've said good-bye to a lot of horses in my time. It's never easy."

"I can handle it, I promise," Rose said quickly. "I'm all right. I want . . . I want to groom him first and make him look good. See, I have his grooming kit."

Uncle Ned nodded. "Not a bad idea."

"I'll bring Star back here and I'll meet you later, Uncle Ned. At the bleachers with my parents and Aunt Norma."

Rose watched Uncle Ned ride off to hitch Monogram up. The field was full of people and horses. She led Star to a water trough. She was surprised by the size of the crowd. The horse fair had to be major entertainment for all the surrounding towns. The smell of frankfurters and buns, introduced at the St. Louis World's Fair only two years before, drifted over the field. A line of children clamored at the pony rides. Rose patted Star. "Easy now," she whispered, to keep him calm in all the confusion. But he'd been a race horse, she thought, so it wasn't new to him. The cloying smell of cotton candy mixed with the odor of manure.

Rose rode to a temporary tent divided into makeshift stalls of canvas and wooden dowels. Rose's yellow entry card gave Star admittance. She led him along a long grass aisle and then, gratefully, she spotted Kat, Amanda, and Lizabeth. They were saving an empty compartment.

Rose dismounted quickly. There was still so much to do!

"I'll pin up your hair," Lizabeth offered.

"I have to check the course first." Rose handed her grooming kit to Kat. "Could you brush him?"

"Don't be long," Amanda said, "It's almost eleven-thirty."

Rose found the show arena. It was surrounded by bleachers. Overhead there was a leftover sign from a Cranberry–North Menasha high school football game. The fences for the jumps were set up and some men were walking the course. Her heart was beating fast. Whoa, she told herself. Don't rush. Focus.

There were twelve jumps altogether, X-jumps and

verticals, mostly the standard two feet and three inches. Jumps four and ten were oxers: two verticals set close together with the height matching the depth, easier than they might look to new riders.

Rose walked through. Most of the fences were well-spaced. She estimated the correct take-off points. Later there'd be no time to think. Rose spoke aloud to help herself memorize the course.

"Three is high, gather him, back well-rounded."

She had to mentally break down the course into a series of three or four jumps, with a beginning, middle, and end, with time for breathing, rebalancing, and turns.

"Five. Jump at an angle to get in position for six." Five was a tricky one! "Change the bend of his body, change the lead as you go over."

Ten, the other oxer. "Tight space between nine and ten. Shorten his stride."

Rose wished she had time for another walk-through. She ran back to the tent, repeating over and over, "Three high, five angle, shorten stride between nine and ten."

Star whinnied to greet her. Kat held the knickers out.

"I'll get Star ready first," Rose said.

She checked his hoofs. Clean. She put a drop of oil on a damp rag and went over his body with long, slow strokes. The glistening dark chestnut coat highlighted his powerful muscles. There was not a speck on his mane or forelock to mar the deep inky black.

Amanda came running into the tent. "Rose, they're calling for the jumpers to line up!"

The other girls blocked the entrance of the canvas stall and Rose changed quickly into the knickers. "Three high, five angle, shorten stride between nine and ten." Amanda fastened the tie around her neck. Lizabeth pinned up her hair, pins scraping against her scalp, and placed the riding hat on top.

Rose led Star out of the tent and mounted. "You and Star," Kat said. "What a team!"

Rose nodded, too frozen to speak. If only she could have arrived at ten o'clock and walked through the course a second time . . .

She started Star on a slow walk on the path to the arena, with Kat, Amanda, and Lizabeth walking by her side. Suddenly her legs nudged Star to a complete halt.

"No," Rose said. She looked at her friends' startled faces. "I can't do this!"

❧ eighteen ❧

T he back of a horse was the one place where Rose had always felt whole, balanced, and comfortable at the very center of her being. But now she was jangling inside, out of tune, pins pulling at her hair, knickers tugging, uneasy in her own skin. Midnight Star stamped and pawed nervously at the ground. He was sensing her discomfort and multiplying it. It was all wrong.

"I can't do this," Rose repeated.

"You can't be *that* scared," Kat said in dismay.

"You've gone to so much trouble," Lizabeth said.

"Don't let stage fright stop you now," Amanda pleaded.

"Oh, I'm *going* to jump," Rose said, "but not in disguise." She dismounted and handed the reins to Kat. She pulled off the tie and riding hat and loosened her hair. "As *myself*! Kat, please hold Star and give me my skirt."

"You can't!" Amanda was shocked. "They won't let you!"

"I have to. This feels too wrong."

"You don't have time," Kat said. "They're calling the first jumper!"

"I'm last, number ten," Rose called over her shoulder as she ran back to the stall. "I can make it." She squirmed out of the knickers and pulled on her divided skirt. The soft, worn leather felt easy and right. She adjusted the riding hat over her free-flowing black mane, and raced back to Star. She mounted. Her pulse was pounding. The worried good wishes of her friends trailed behind her and she nudged the horse into a trot.

"It's you and me now, Star," she whispered into his mane. "It's up to us."

Rose and Star entered the arena and joined the line of other horses and riders waiting to compete. A man with a megaphone guarded the entry gate. She scanned the crowd sitting in the bleachers. Momma and Poppa, Aunt Norma and Uncle Ned. She saw Kat, Amanda, and Lizabeth rushing through the benches to join them.

"Number Six," the official shouted into the megaphone. "Alan Montgomery, riding Sterling!"

Rose watched the gray mare and her rider take the

warm-up trot around the arena and then canter to the first fence. Sterling's approach was enthusiastic, but she didn't have much spring in her jumps. The mare was trying hard, but she didn't always get her hind legs out of the way in time to avoid brushing the top rail of the fence. Rose felt for Sterling. All heart but not much talent.

"Number Seven! John Stevens, riding Bluebonnet!" A solid display of good horsemanship.

"Number Eight! Daniel Albright, riding Thunder-cloud!" A good start, but they slowed down on the approach to jump five—the worst thing the rider could do. Maybe he was worried about the angle coming up. It resulted in Thundercloud's refusal and then—

The gatekeeper interrupted Rose's thoughts. "Sorry miss, you have to move out of the way."

"Pardon me?"

"You can't stay here. You're in the way of the jumpers."

"I *am* a jumper!" Rose handed him her entry card. "Number Ten. R. L., that's me. Rose Lorraine Forbes riding Midnight Star."

He looked her over. His expression went from befuddlement to irritation. "That's impossible! No girls!" He put the megaphone to his mouth. "Number Nine. Bill

Laramie, riding Sweet Caroline!"

"I'm sorry, sir, but that's my entry card, my *official* entry card, and I'm up next!"

"Don't make trouble, miss. Now move along!" He took Star's reins in his hand and tugged.

"*Don't touch my horse.*" Rose's voice was pure steel; Star started to rear. "I'm jumping! I'm Number Ten and *nothing* and *no one* is going to stop me now!"

Is that *me* speaking? Rose marveled. She was throwing all her fears away!

The gatekeeper's face reddened. Maybe it was the threat in Rose's glittering black eyes, or perhaps he decided he didn't want to be trampled by a massive chestnut horse, or maybe he simply wished to avoid a scene. He dropped the reins and looked around for another official to handle the problem, but he seemed to be alone.

Number Ten!" he finally called through the megaphone.

"*Rose Lorraine* Forbes," Rose prompted.

"Rose Lorraine Forbes, riding Midnight Star!"

Rose and Star rode around the arena in a warm-up trot. She heard the surprised gasp from the crowd and then the hostile buzz all around her. "A *girl*?" "That's indecent!" "What in the world is she wearing?" She could see the frowns and outraged faces. But then only one came into perfect focus: Momma with a proud, radiant smile. The others became a blur. Even when Rose turned in the circle and could no longer see Momma, her proud, encouraging smile was in her mind's eye.

The warm-up ride was completed; they sped up to a canter. The noise from the crowd fell away. Rose heard nothing but Star's hoofbeats, saw nothing but the fences ahead, thought of nothing but the first jump. This was where she needed to establish rhythm and attitude for the entire course. She was ready for the take-off point eight strides early and moved her body forward in half-seat. Star's front feet struck the ground for the last time, his back rounded, and he pushed off with his hind legs. Star, glistening in the sunlight, flew over the first fence with the grace and power of a great athlete.

Then the other fences came, one after another, at breathtaking speed. Jump two, jump three—the high one—jump four. Rose's concentration was total: remember to breathe, look ahead never down, maintain control, sit in the saddle between jumps. . . . Jump five—the angle, Star's body curving around Rose's leg. Six, seven, eight. Star cleared the fences as lightly and gracefully as a deer bounding through a meadow. Tight space between nine and ten, shorten his stride, a lighter seat, a sharper motion with her legs, hands set more firmly. Ten, eleven.

Finally, twelve—the last one. Ride it as though there were thirteen, Rose thought. Don't let down with relief because it's the last or speed up with excitement about being almost finished.

And then it was over. Star ran out in a canter for a few strides and Rose slowed him to a trot. She led him out of the showring and into a cooldown turn around the arena. It was only then that normal sounds and sights came back to her consciousness. Still a buzz, but the tone had changed. She looked up at the stands. Kat, Amanda, and Lizabeth were standing up and cheering, clapping their hands high over their heads. Uncle Ned was rushing down, climbing over benches. Rose heard other words from the spectators now, good words about her horsemanship mixed in with the disapproval.

She dismounted and ran her hand over Star. He was damp with sweat. If she had done well, Rose thought, it was only because she didn't get in Midnight Star's way. She'd never know if it was natural talent or if he'd been trained for jumps. He knew intuitively what to do. He could feel not only her physical clues and her slightest gesture, but she was sure he could feel her thinking, too. She had never been in such perfect harmony with anyone. She put her head against his neck. "We did everything we could, Star. I don't know what happens next." How could they possibly part now?

Uncle Ned and Aunt Norma, Momma and Poppa, Kat, Lizabeth, and Amanda crowded around her.

"Rose, I'm bowled over. I had no idea—he was brilliant," Uncle Ned said. "You both were!"

"I didn't know for sure myself," Rose admitted. "I thought he was good, but it wasn't until we were actually on the course . . . Uncle Ned, he's special, isn't he?" She hesitated to ask the next question: Can Star please stay at Clayton Stables? She was afraid of the answer. She was bracing herself to ask when she was interrupted by the announcements.

They all turned to listen. "Third place, John Stevens, riding Bluebonnet! Second place, Tom Young, riding Lucky Guess. First place, Rose Lorraine Forbes, riding Midnight Star!"

A blue ribbon! Everyone was excited for her, and, of course, she was, too. But what did a blue ribbon mean to Star? All a horse needs is kindness and patience and proper care, Rose thought. If Star had to be sold, maybe a blue ribbon would allow them to be picky about the buyer. Maybe he could go to a girl just like herself, who would love him as much as she did.

Momma and Poppa hugged her. "Imagine, first place!" Poppa said. "And as *Rose Lorraine* Forbes," Momma added. She and Rose shared a proud smile.

Rose noticed a gentleman in a pearl gray suit and a dark beard near them. He was walking around Star and looking him over very carefully. It made Rose uncomfortable. He approached Uncle Ned, and Rose moved closer to them.

"I'm interested in buying your horse," the gentleman said.

Rose's heart clutched. She looked into his eyes. Was he a good man? She couldn't tell.

Uncle Ned didn't answer immediately. Was he also looking for signs of kindness in the stranger?

"He's a fine jumper. He belongs on the circuit," the gentleman continued. "I'll give you a fair price. What do you want for him?"

What was "the circuit"? Would Star be used—and abused—for his ability, the way he had been when he was a racehorse? Rose was so afraid for him. She had meant to be mature about this, but she couldn't, she *couldn't.* She'd run away with Star, she'd mount and gallop away! Her hand clutched the saddle. *Now!*

"You'll have to ask his owner," Uncle Ned said, and gestured toward Rose. She looked at her uncle in confusion. With a smile, he handed the transfer of ownership form to her. Incredibly, her name was written in under NEW OWNER! She blinked and looked at it again. For a long moment, she couldn't take in the meaning of it. Then tears ran from her eyes.

The gentleman turned to her. "Well?" he said impatiently.

Rose pulled herself together. "He's not for sale, sir, not at any price." The most wonderful words she had ever spoken!

With one look at her, the gentleman recognized there was no point in making an offer. He shrugged and walked away.

"Thank you, Uncle Ned! Thank you!"

"You both earned my respect. . . . " Uncle Ned cleared his throat. "I'm thinking you and Star could give jumping demonstrations at Clayton Stables. Or help train beginning jumpers. Something new for my students."

"I'd be glad to, Uncle Ned. Thank you!" Rose said. "This is easily the best day of my life!"

Kat, Amanda, and Lizabeth beamed as they realized what had happened. Rose hugged each one of them. "I couldn't have done it without help from my friends!"

Rose tore herself away from their warm embraces. She had a horse to take care of. *Her* horse! "Star needs to be watered and wiped down," she said. "I'll meet you here later for the dressage events."

She led Star past the busy concession stands and toward the water trough. Several people frowned at her divided skirt. One woman pointed and tsk-tsked. But a gentleman passing by said, "That was a fine ride, young lady." And a young couple smiled at her. "Congratulations, you certainly deserved first place!" Rose walked with her head held high. Perhaps competence was winning out over costume.

I have no control over what people think, good or bad. I can only control my own behavior, Rose thought. And I have to be true to myself. Just like Momma!

"Good job, R. L.," said a deep voice at her elbow.

Christopher Merchant!

"That *was* you, wasn't it? At the Cranberry station yesterday?"

What could she do but nod? "How . . . how did you know?" Maybe he was disgusted by a girl whom he had seen in boys' clothes!

He raised his eyebrows, and his eyes had an amused gleam as he pointed. "My shirt?"

"Oh. Yes. I'm sorry." It was wrinkled and soiled by now. "I'll have it washed and ironed. Your tie, too."

"So you're Rose Lorraine Forbes from Lighthouse Lane." He had the *nicest* smile! "You know, I didn't recognize my shirt at first. But I couldn't miss those flashing gypsy eyes."

Oh! That was exactly what Poppa said when he talked about falling in love with Momma!

He winked. "See you later, Rose Lorraine."

Could any day be more perfect?

≈≈≈

That evening, Rose and Midnight Star rode along Lighthouse Lane in the white glow of moonlight. Rose was going to meet Kat, Amanda, and Lizabeth in the lighthouse tower, where they would rehash and celebrate the events of this wonderful day.

The clear night sky was studded with stars, but even the north star didn't shine as brilliantly as the lighthouse beacon.

I'm no longer the frightened, plain girl who moved to Cape Light just a little while ago, Rose thought. And

Midnight Star is no longer the isolated, tense horse that was brought to Clayton Stables. "It's a fresh, new start for both of us," she whispered into Midnight Star's inky mane. "Thank you, God, for helping us find the way."

They rode through the soft spring night, and the light from the tower guided their path.